"Tell me you forgot me," he ordered, his voice harsh.

"No." The admission came out like a sigh, softly languorous, silken with need and longing.

At last, she thought with a relief so intense it blocked out everything but delight. *At last.*

She had been waiting for this ever since— ever since she'd seen him standing in the doorway.

Waiting for Luke.

The shock of realization sent a rush of sensation through her, tightening her breasts and heating the pit of her stomach. For a few stunned seconds she stayed immobile, until the reality of everything hit her in an elemental, all-consuming flood, weakening her knees so that she swayed into him.

He understood the silent surrender, bending his head so she felt the soft whisper of his words against her sensitized lips. "Good. Because I could not forget you."

ROBYN DONALD

Greetings! I'm often asked what made me decide to be a writer of romances. Well, it wasn't so much a decision as an inevitable conclusion. Growing up in a family of readers helped. After anxious calls from neighbors driving our dusty country road, my mother tried to persuade me to wait until I got home before I started reading the current library book, but the lure of those pages was always too strong.

Shortly after I started school I started whispering stories in the dark to my two sisters. Although most of those tales bore a remarkable resemblance to whatever book I was immersed in, there were times when a new idea would pop into my brain—my first experience of the joy of creativity.

Growing up in New Zealand, in the subtropical north, gave me a taste for romantic landscapes and exotic gardens. But it wasn't until I was in my mid-twenties that I read a Harlequin romance and realized that the country I love came alive when populated by strong, tough men and spirited women.

By then I was married and a working mother, but into my busy life I crammed hours of writing; my family has always been hugely supportive, even the various dogs who have slept on my feet and demanded that I take them for walks at inconvenient times. I learned my craft in those busy years, and when I finally plucked up enough courage to send off a manuscript, it was accepted. The only thing I can compare that excitement to is the delight of bearing a child.

Since then it's been a roller-coaster ride of fun and hard work and wonderful letters from fans. I see my readers as intelligent women who insist on accurate backgrounds as well as an intriguing love story, so I spend time researching as well as writing.

POWERFUL GREEK, HOUSEKEEPER WIFE

ROBYN DONALD

~ The Greek Tycoons ~

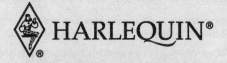

HARLEQUIN®

TORONTO • NEW YORK • LONDON
AMSTERDAM • PARIS • SYDNEY • HAMBURG
STOCKHOLM • ATHENS • TOKYO • MILAN • MADRID
PRAGUE • WARSAW • BUDAPEST • AUCKLAND

Recycling programs
for this product may
not exist in your area.

ISBN-13: 978-0-373-52785-4

POWERFUL GREEK, HOUSEKEEPER WIFE

First North American Publication 2010.

Copyright © 2010 by Robyn Donald.

This is a work of fiction. Names, characters, places and incidents are
either the product of the author's imagination or are used fictitiously,
and any resemblance to actual persons, living or dead, business
establishments, events or locales is entirely coincidental.

This edition published by arrangement with Harlequin Books S.A.

For questions and comments about the quality of this book
please contact us at Customer_eCare@Harlequin.ca.

www.eHarlequin.com

Printed in U.S.A.

POWERFUL GREEK,
HOUSEKEEPER WIFE

CHAPTER ONE

IONA GUTHRIE bit back an unladylike expletive and tore off her wet smock, wrinkling her nose at the disgusting stickiness of the liquid that oozed down her front and soaked her to the skin.

'*Now* what?' she demanded of the universe, heading for the elegant little powder room close by the entrance of the penthouse. 'First the vacuum system dies, then the laundry loses the special linen, probably produced by diamond-decorated silkworms. Now this—ugh! I'm beginning to believe this penthouse is haunted by a demon. So what's next? An earthquake? A waterspout?'

She pushed back the thick strand of straight ash-blonde hair that had come adrift from her businesslike ponytail, and opened the door. Grimacing, she slung the smock over a towel rail and began to wriggle free of her bra. The scent of the roses in the exquisitely arranged vase permeated the luxurious little room, calming her down a little.

How the other half—no, make that the upper point zero zero zero one per cent—live, she thought, glancing at the flowers.

Fortunately the billionaire businessman for whom the penthouse had been prepared wasn't due to arrive for several hours yet.

And she'd almost finished the checklist. Iona made a mental note to tell the manager of the apartment complex that the maid needed supervision; one of the hand basins in the master bedroom suite had had a hair in it. She'd picked up the detergent bottle to clean it, only to discover that the lid hadn't been put on properly.

The view from the window was enough to soothe anyone, even a detergent-soaked lifestyle organiser. Relaxing into the promise of a sunny weekend, Auckland city hummed peacefully below. A warm spring sun beamed down, highlighting the white wakes of pleasure boats on the harbour and gilding islands that faded into the distance.

Iona expelled another long breath and finally managed to shrug free of the loathsomely sticky bra, glancing at her watch when a muted *ting* from the communications system warned her that the private lift was on its way up.

Good for you, Angie. Dead on time. Her cousin, who was also her boss, was collecting her for the next job, a barbecue one of her clients had suddenly decided to hold that evening.

Her bra landed on the towel rail next to her soggy smock. Pulling a face at her half-naked reflection, she extracted a handful of tissues from her bag before turning on the elegant Italian tap.

She heard the big outer doors slide back, and called out, 'Come on in,' as she began to mop the residue of the detergent from her skin.

A moment later she sensed Angie's presence. Dabbing distastefully at her bare breasts, she said, 'I won't be long.'

'You'd damned well better not be.'

Iona froze. Not Angie—*definitely* not Angie.

Deep, slightly accented, very much male—a voice chilled by a contempt that sent slivers of ice jostling down her spine.

And familiar...oh, so familiar. That voice still haunted her dreams.

Her head jerked up. In the mirror her stunned gaze met eyes like a lion's—tawny and arrogantly disdainful in a bold masculine face.

A man straight out of a Greek fable.

Or a Tahitian fantasy...

A shocked sound tore from Iona's throat when she registered the starkly classic beauty of his features. She swallowed, then croaked, *'Luke?'*

'What the hell are you doing here?' Luke Michelakis asked in a voice so cold it froze her brain.

Hot colour washed up from her naked breasts as she grabbed at the discarded smock and wrapped it around her, only to see her bra slither onto the floor. 'I was—I'm checking the place over,' she muttered. She dragged in a jagged breath and demanded, 'Why are you here?'

'I'm staying here,' he said icily.

'You are?' she blurted, heart pounding so heavily in her chest she was afraid he might hear it. Indignation sharpened her tone. 'Well, you're not due for another five hours!'

Black brows lifted. For a disturbing few seconds he let his unreadable gaze roam her face, then he stooped, picked up the bra and held it out to her, skin-coloured cotton dangling from a long-fingered olive hand.

'Th-thank you.' She snatched the offending scrap of material and tried to regain some shred of dignity. 'Please go.'

The black lashes drooping over those exotic eyes

couldn't hide a glitter that sent a shameful shiver through Iona.

Nothing of that gleam of awareness showed in his tone when he drawled, 'Gladly.'

Humiliated, she turned away. Not that there was any refuge—the mirrored walls revealed every inch of her shrinking, exposed skin to his scathing survey.

For a taut, hugely embarrassing second it seemed he was going to stand there and watch her dress.

She said harshly, 'Go now!'

'My pleasure,' he bit out, and left with the lithe, silent menace of a predator.

Weak from shock and relief, Iona slammed and locked the door behind him, then seized the wet bra and struggled back into it. Her bones felt like rubber and she had to draw several difficult breaths before the colour returned to her skin and she could think clearly.

From the moment they'd met, Lukas Michelakis had had that effect on her—he literally took her breath away.

Charisma, she thought wildly. *Presence, impact*—whatever the term, Luke possessed it in spades. Eighteen months previously it had been the first thing she'd noticed when he'd strode towards her across pristine sands in Tahiti—that, and the authority with which he'd ordered her off, telling her the beach was private.

Luke—here in New Zealand. *He* was the man she and Angie had cheerfully referred to as the unknown plutocrat.

This penthouse *had* to be possessed by a demon, and it had set her up nicely. It was probably laughing its evil head off.

She'd just scrambled back into her smock when the doorbell pealed again.

Oh, at last—Angie...

And no sign of Luke as she hurtled out and opened the door. But instead of the calm presence of her cousin, she was confronted by a harried apartment maid holding a bag.

'The linen from the laundry,' she informed Iona, eyes widening as she looked past her.

Bracing herself, Iona turned. Tall and tigerish, darkly dominating, Luke paced silently towards them.

'I'll show you the rooms to be made up,' Iona said swiftly. Holding her shoulders so stiffly they protested, she almost frog-marched the maid down the corridor towards the three bedrooms.

'Who's the guy?' the other woman hissed just before Iona left.

'A guest of the owner,' Iona said crisply.

'He can be my guest any time he likes,' the girl growled, then giggled.

Iona left the room, unconsciously walking quietly. To no avail; a grim-faced Luke appeared and said curtly, 'I need to talk to you. Come with me.'

Her spine tingled, every nerve in her body sending out a red alert. Ignoring a foolhardy impulse to announce that she didn't take orders from him, she assembled the tatters of her composure and looked up to meet his hooded, intent gaze.

A dangerous move, she thought in dismay when her body suffused with heat.

It took every scrap of control she could produce to steady her voice. 'I'm sorry the bedrooms aren't made up, but the laundry managed to lose the sheets. They've just arrived.'

A negligent shrug of broad shoulders informed her he wasn't interested. He said, 'I can still see a sticky trail of something on your skin. You'd better finish cleaning up, then I want to see you on the terrace.' He paused, his expression unreadable, before drawling, 'I can lend you a shirt if you want one.'

Once—in Tahiti—he'd slung his shirt around her when her shoulders started to burn in the sun, and its removal had led to an erotic interlude that came surging back into her mind only too vividly.

Of course he knew. Colour burned across her cheekbones, and he lifted an arrogant eyebrow, his eyes narrowing in sardonic challenge.

'That won't be necessary,' Iona said, before swinging on her heel and heading back into the powder room. She locked the door behind her, leaned back against it and bit her lip.

Arrogant? Forcing herself to move, she wiped off the detergent.

Arrogant was far too insipid a word to describe Luke Michelakis. She ran her fingers through her hair in a vain attempt to restore its sleekness, and listed words much better suited to the man—words like *cynical*, *dominating*, and *intimidating*...

It was a satisfying exercise, but she couldn't concentrate on it. Different, infinitely dangerous words refused to budge from her brain.

Sexy. Magnetic. Compelling.

And those words were why eighteen months previously on a hot, deserted beach in Tahiti she'd made the craziest decision in her life. One look at Luke Michelakis had told her he was just what she needed—a man vibrant with charisma, his personality vital enough to rescue her from the emotional desolation that had followed the death of her fiancé, followed soon afterwards by the car crash that took both her parents.

Instinct had whispered that this magnetic Greek would know exactly how to bring her back to life. He'd know how to make a woman scream in rapture— and in his arms, in his bed, she'd feel safe as well as pleasured.

That same perverse instinct had also been sure that because he was handsome and arrogantly sure of himself, he wouldn't want anything more than an affair.

Instinct—while perfectly correct—hadn't known the half of it, Iona thought grimly. Luke had not only introduced her to a sensual intensity she'd never imagined, he'd converted what should have been a very temporary fling into an experience that had changed her life. In his arms she'd learned just how wonderful a superb lover could make a woman feel.

And that erotic discovery had backfired big time, bringing bitter guilt. Gavin had died to save her life; she'd mourned him so deeply she'd been hovering on the edge of depression, yet somehow in ten days and nights of passion Luke took not just her body but a piece of her heart. Disgusted with herself, she'd fled Tahiti, determined to banish all memories of the time she'd spent there.

It hadn't worked, and now here Luke was in New Zealand. Of all the *wretched* coincidences!

It should comfort her that once she got out of this penthouse they wouldn't see each other again. Except that his appearance—so unexpected, so embarrassing— had lit fires she'd thought long smothered.

Iona rinsed out her bra, wrung it free of surplus water and put it back on again. Her body heat would soon have it dry. The smock still clung, and she was acutely aware of her breasts beneath it, of skin so sensitive the material seemed to drag against it, of heat burgeoning deep inside her. She took a deep breath before walking steadily out into the hall with her head held high and what felt like a herd of buffaloes rampaging through her stomach.

The hall was empty, but not for long. Silently, his handsome face grim, Luke came pacing through from the drawing room.

Luke watched Iona come towards him, the lights gilding the cool ash-blonde of her hair. Although it had been a year and half since he'd last seen her, everything about her was burnt into his brain—the warmth of her sleek body, the dark mystery of her changeable blue-green eyes, the lush promise of her mouth...

Her wild surrender.

And his searing feeling of betrayal when she'd walked out on him, the conflict that raged between his prized, iron-clad control and a primal awareness that his affair with Iona had been something rare, much more intense than mere holiday madness.

For the first time Luke admitted that one of the reasons he'd come to New Zealand was to see if he could contact her again. Just to make sure she was all right, of course.

He hadn't expected to find her within a couple of hours of landing. His over-developed sense of responsibility should be satisfied because she was obviously fine.

And certainly not filled with delight to see him again.

But she was still very, very conscious of him.

Setting aside the potent, inconvenient pleasure of that realisation, he said abruptly, 'It will be best if we talk out of earshot of the maid.'

Iona had resolved to treat him with cool detachment, and in a matching tone she managed, 'Very well.'

As he escorted her out onto the terrace she realised anew just how lithe he was. Tall, broad-shouldered, he walked with the prowling, noiseless grace of some great beast of prey.

Not the sort of man anyone would ever overlook.

Once out on the terrace, blocked from the sounds of the city by lush plantings, without ceremony he demanded, 'What are you doing here?'

'I'm making sure that the apartment is ready for you and your party,' she said with an attempt at cool detachment.

A black brow climbed. 'Your employer appears to be a little too trusting. You left the door unlocked—anyone could have come in.'

Iona suspected he was waiting for a defensive response. Well, she wasn't going to give it to him.

Crisply she replied, 'The security here is excellent. The bell sounds when the elevator is stopping at this floor, and as you were supposed to arrive much later this afternoon I assumed it was my employer—Ms Makepeace—who'd been let in by the concierge.'

He dismissed her words with another hard-eyed stare. 'I gather she is not the housekeeper.'

He couldn't possibly be interested in domestic arrangements. This wasn't even his apartment; one of Angie's clients was lending it to Luke while he was in New Zealand. Was he getting some small-minded amusement from emphasising the distance between them?

After all, in Tahiti she'd walked out on him. It had probably never happened to him before.

Or since.

But the man she'd known had not been small-minded. Repressing a rush of too-poignant memories, she replied, 'You're right, she's not the housekeeper. She owns and runs a business organising the lives of people too busy to do it themselves.'

'In other words, a housekeeper and butler service,' he observed on a note of irony.

Iona gave him her best, kindest, nursery-school-teacher smile. 'More like a manager,' she corrected. 'She's extremely successful—hugely discreet, one hundred per cent dependable, and a perfectionist. Your host asked us to make sure the apartment was ready for you, so I called in this morning to check it out. Unfortunately there were a few minor problems, which are on the way to being fixed now. If you'd arrived at the time you said you would, everything would have been perfect.'

He gave a sudden crack of laughter, and for a moment he was the man she'd known, the man she'd fallen—well, not in love with. No, *never* that.

In lust with.

Amusement didn't soften the autocratic lines and angles of Luke's face, but it did make him more approachable when he said lazily, 'It was convenient for me to arrive early. The rest of my party will be here at the given time.'

Going by the bedrooms she'd checked there were at least two other people to come. Was he planning to share that big bed with someone? A stupid pang of pain seared through Iona, as though the possibility was a kind of betrayal.

Startled and afraid, she said briskly, 'All that needs to be done now is for the beds to be made. And if you'll excuse me, I'll go and help the maid and then you'll have the apartment to yourself.'

'It is not necessary,' he said negligently, eyes intent. A slow smile curled his beautifully chiselled mouth. 'I am in no hurry to see you go. Tell me how you've been since you left Tahiti so swiftly.'

This was exactly the sort of thing ex-lovers might say to each other when they were being civilised and sensible and sophisticated about a past affair.

Well, she was just as capable as Luke of being all those things—perhaps not quite so sophisticated...

Yet it took a considerable amount of control for Iona to say as casually, 'I've been fine, thank you.'

'You didn't go back to teaching your little nursery school pupils?'

'No. I was offered this position.'

She knew she sounded stiff, but she couldn't be as relaxed as he was. Apart from Gavin he was the only man she'd ever made love to, but, more than that, his heated, generously sensual expertise had drawn her back into the world of the living, the world of emotions and joy and the ability to respond. He'd got too close to her during those passionate days and nights in Tahiti.

She flicked a glance up at him, noting the glimmer of amusement in the tawny eyes. A strange constriction of her heart took her by surprise, as though she'd spent the intervening months waiting for this moment.

It had to be his powerful physical presence. Luke was the best-looking man she'd ever seen, but that wasn't why her throat had dried. He was so much more than the strong, thrusting bone structure that framed his features, the beautiful lines of the mouth that had given her so much pleasure, the strong, elegant hands...

He interrupted her thoughts with another question. 'And you enjoy managing other people's lives for them?'

'Very much, thank you,' she said sedately.

Obviously she was only too eager to get the hell out of there. Luke fought back an unexpected spurt of temper. He wasn't foolish enough to fall in love with his mistresses; experience had taught him not to let down his guard. So Iona's calm lack of warmth should not only reassure him that she was in control of her life, but allow him to snap the tenuous bonds of an insignificant affair.

Instead he found himself resisting a wild impulse to touch her.

Alarm bells should be screaming, yet it took every shred of self-control not to reach out to her, run the tip of his forefinger around the luscious curve of her top lip, and then down the pale line of her throat, watch her changeable eyes darken into desire.

To prove she was no more immune to him than he was to her…

The doorbell rang. Iona started, then stepped back, blinking shadowed eyes. Luke felt as though he'd been poised on the edge of some dangerous precipice, and realised savagely that he'd just been about to make an idiot of himself.

She swivelled and said huskily, 'That's probably Angie—my employer.'

Luke's voice was cold and deliberate, chilling her right through. 'I'll come with you.'

It was Angie. Iona hoped Luke didn't notice the flicker of unease in the older woman's expression.

It was masked by the calm professionalism in her tone when she said, 'I'm Angela Makepeace; you must be one of the guests expected here?'

'Yes. I am Lukas Michelakis.'

Angie held out her hand. 'How do you do? I'm sorry,

Mr Michelakis, but we were told you wouldn't be here until late this afternoon.'

Somewhat to Iona's surprise Luke accepted the courtesy, long tanned fingers enveloping Angie's in a brisk shake. 'As you see, I am early,' he said, as though it were explanation enough.

Angie nodded, and went on, 'I assume you've met Iona?'

'Iona and I already knew each other,' he said without expression.

Angie's glance swivelled to Iona's still face, then back to the dark countenance of the man towering over her. 'What a coincidence,' she said uncertainly.

'An amazing one.'

Angry at being talked about as though she weren't there, Iona said abruptly, 'The beds should be made up by now—I'll just go and check.'

As she turned away she heard Luke say, 'I wish to speak to you, Ms Makepeace.'

Angie's reply was muffled as they moved towards the drawing room. Questions buzzed around Iona's mind. Why did he want to talk to her cousin?

And what had happened in that final intense moment when his gaze had dropped to her lips and tension had drummed between them, an insistent beat that drowned out every sensible thought in her mind?

Forget it, she told herself angrily, and checked the first and second bedroom. The maid had just finished making up the big king-size one in the master suite; she looked up as Iona came in and gave a swift smile. 'All done.'

'Thank you,' Iona said as she slipped into the bathroom to make sure it was free of any trace of spilt detergent.

It was clear, and she'd just emerged from the suite when she heard her cousin call her name. Angie was on her own.

'He's on the phone, and it's looking good,' Angie said softly. 'We might be put on retainer while he's staying in New Zealand. Why is your smock wet?'

Hurriedly Iona explained, ending, 'I hope you've got a spare one in the car?'

'Yep.' She handed over the keys. 'Your Lukas hoped so too.'

'He's not my Lukas!' He'd never corrected her when she'd called him Luke.

Angie grinned. 'Go down and get the smock from the back seat, then get changed here.' Reading Iona's instinctive objection she said, 'It's OK—he suggested it. I'm waiting while he runs a check on the business.'

'What?'

'He's a very rich man,' Angie said with a shrug. 'They're not into trust. Off you go.'

When Iona got back with the clean smock she heard the sound of voices in the drawing room, and hastily shot into the powder room, gratefully pulled the crisp dry garment on and, after stuffing the wet one into her bag, examined the room to make sure it was pristine.

'Good, not a rose petal out of place,' she muttered, and came through the door, stopping abruptly when she met Luke's eyes.

One eyebrow lifted, and his smile was brief as he said, 'You look much more comfortable.'

'Thanks for letting me use the room.'

That eyebrow cocked again, giving him a sardonic air. Hard eyes fixed on her face, as though he could read both her thoughts and the emotions rioting through her, he asked, 'Are you and your employer sisters?'

Iona's surprise must have shown because his broad shoulders lifted in a slight shrug. 'Your colouring is different, but the shape of your face is identical to hers. The curve of your lips also, as well as a certain silken texture to your skin.'

His sculpted mouth curled in a narrow smile, and after a deliberate pause that set her nerves jangling he said lazily, 'I have never forgotten it.'

Sensation prickled along her nerves, pooled inside her, reminding her of the bold, masculine virility that had swept her into an affair that now seemed like a dangerous fantasy.

It took all of her self-control to be able to say shortly, 'We're cousins.'

CHAPTER TWO

GOING down in the lift, Angie said, 'Where did you meet him, and why haven't I heard about it?'

Iona had been bracing herself for questions, but even so, she paused as the lift came to a halt in the basement car park. 'We met in Tahiti,' she said, keeping her tone casual and matter-of-fact. 'On the second anniversary of Gavin's death. I was walking along a deserted beach—'

'Wallowing in grief and guilt, I bet,' Angie said astringently. 'Iona, nobody knew Gavin had a heart weakness. Yes, saving you exhausted him and he drowned, but it was an unexpected, shocking tragedy, not your fault.'

Iona said quietly, 'Intellectually I knew that, but I just couldn't accept it.'

Angie unlocked the car and got in. Once they were settled she said, 'And then your parents were killed by that damned drunk driver. It's no wonder you were a mess. Then you met Lukas Michelakis in Tahiti?'

'Yes. Actually when he strode down the beach—like—like the king of the gods—to inform me I was trespassing I was actually *relieved*. He gave me something else to think about.' With a vengeance.

Once they were under way, Angie said, 'And what happened then?'

'We went around a bit together,' Iona told her in a flat voice, 'until I came home again.'

'And you haven't been in contact since?' Angie asked.

'There was no reason.'

Her cousin took the hint. 'I read somewhere that he grew up in a very wealthy family.'

'It figures,' Iona said evenly. 'His kind of confidence is bred in the genes.'

'The article was cagey, but heavy on innuendo—obviously making sure no lawyer could sue the writer or the newspaper. It implied something pretty disastrous happened when he was young—late teens, perhaps?—and he left home to strike out on his own.'

'Probably with the family's support not too far in the background.' Iona didn't try to hide the cynical note in her words.

'I doubt if he needed it. It didn't take him long to turn into an internet czar.' Angie paused before asking casually, 'If he needs to call on us, how would you feel about working with him?'

'Me?' Iona swallowed an unnecessary panic. 'A bit self-conscious, that's all. I was half-naked, mopping detergent off my breasts, when he strode in like a clap of doom just before you arrived, and I suspect he thought it was a set-up—that I'd deliberately stripped to attract his attention.'

'I suppose it's happened before,' Angie said, and gave her a thoughtful sideways glance. 'I bet he spends a fair part of his life swatting off importunate women.'

During their brief affair he'd more than met Iona halfway.

Repressing disturbing images of tropical folly, she said hastily, 'I'll be fine. He relaxed when you turned up.'

Although *relaxed* wasn't the word to describe Luke. Even on holiday she'd sensed a leashed, prowling awareness in him, an uncompromising authority that made him both formidable and intimidating.

It was still there, intensified by an ironic detachment she'd not experienced before.

Get over it, she told herself. She still resented the hard contempt of his gaze in the powder room, but that was good, because resentment was a much safer emotion than sighing lustfully after him.

The barbecue Angie had been asked to organise only the day before went on until after midnight and they were both tired when at last they left the beach house an hour's drive north of Auckland.

Covering a yawn, Iona said, 'I wish someone would persuade Mrs Parker not to throw any more impromptu parties. I suppose we should have guessed her few close friends would morph into about fifty.'

'She'll be paying heavily for springing it on us at such short notice. Besides, it's work, and we need it,' Angie said practically.

After a tentative moment Iona asked, 'How are things?'

Her cousin paused before admitting, 'You've probably guessed the recession's making inroads into the client list, but we're surviving.' Her tone changed. 'If there's an emergency in the next two days, can I call on you? The boys are going to a birthday party tomorrow—well, actually it will be today—and tomorrow we're going to the zoo.'

'Of course. Give me the work phone,' Iona said. 'If I need you I'll ring you on your personal phone. You need a break and the boys need time with you.'

It took some persuading, but at last she managed to convince Angie to agree.

Inside her tiny studio flat Iona showered and dropped into bed. Sleep came quickly, bringing with it images of a tall, dark man, images that led to dreams. Eventually she woke in a state of high excitement, blood racing through her veins, her body racked by a feverish desire.

Grim-faced and desperate, she willed her heart to settle down and her body to relax. That was how it had started. Tahiti was everything the brochures had promised—wildly, sensuously exotic, filled with beautiful people of both sexes, scented by flowers and lapped by a brilliant turquoise sea, alive with the sound of music and drums and laughter, the hush of waves on the lagoon shores. The glorious islands throbbed with life.

Iona had looked, but been unable to enjoy. Grief had dulled her senses so completely she'd felt totally disconnected from everything.

And then she'd met Luke—Lukas. She'd had no idea who—or what—he was. The moment her gaze clashed with his lion eyes, sensations she'd believed had died for ever had suddenly flared into life, introducing her to hope. A flare of conscious response had set her nerves tingling and heated her body, sharpening her senses so that the world suddenly blazed into a glory of colour and sound and sensuous delight.

Why had he pursued her? She'd asked him once, and he'd laughed.

'Perhaps the thrill of the chase,' he admitted without shame. 'You looked at me with such cool disdain, as though I was less interesting to you than the shell in your hand. I wondered what it would be like to see desire in those intriguing blue-green mermaid's eyes, as changeable and mysterious as the sea.'

For some foolish reason his words hurt. She covered the momentary stab of pain with a smile, and slid her arms around him. 'And has it lived up to your expectations?'

His gaze kindled, golden flames dancing in the depths. 'More than I ever expected; it's infinitely fascinating to watch. And even more fascinating to experience,' he said in a low growl, and kissed her.

Lost in swift passion, she'd kissed him back, welcoming the hot tide of hunger that met and matched his.

Their passionate, hedonistic affair had seemed so right in Tahiti, christened Aphrodite's Isles by the first dazzled European sailors to visit those idyllic shores.

Then one night, as the moon came up over the horizon in a splendour of silver and gold, he'd said, 'I'm leaving in three days.' He had smiled lazily at her startled face and kissed the curve of her breast, murmuring against her skin, 'Come with me.'

Each word had been a caress—a confident one. He'd had no doubt she'd do what he wanted. The fantasy world Iona had been living in crashed around her.

'I can't,' she said, shocked by a swift, aching temptation to give him what he wanted.

His eyes narrowed, focused on her face as intently as a hunter's scrutiny. 'Why?'

'Because this has been—wonderful, but we both know it's not real life.' It was surprisingly hard to say, but his words had awakened the common sense she'd abandoned the moment her eyes had met his.

He shrugged again and replied, 'It could be.' And when she remained silent, he said a little impatiently,

'I will, of course, look after you—make sure you don't lose anything by being with me.'

Knowing what he was offering, she almost flinched. For a while she'd be his lover; while she was with him she'd exist in this sensual dream.

And when it was over she'd go back to New Zealand with memories...

And the possibility of more grief. She'd had enough of that in her life. 'No,' she said.

He'd laughed deep in his throat and slid down her body, his mouth questing as he tasted her sleek skin.

Later, when she was quivering with passionate exhaustion in his arms, he murmured, 'I'm going to enjoy making you change your mind.'

But, back in her own bed at the hotel, she'd dreamed of Gavin and woke weeping. And when she slipped out early to walk along the white sands, she forced herself to face a few unpleasant facts.

Without realising it, she'd selfishly used Luke. Oh, he'd made it obvious from the start that he intended nothing more than a sexual relationship, but that didn't make her feel any better.

Her swift, reckless surrender to overwhelming passion had betrayed and tarnished the love she'd shared with Gavin. She tried to conjure up the emotions she'd felt for her fiancé, but against the blazing intensity of her relationship with Luke he seemed faded and shadowy, a lovely memory but no longer the foundation of her life.

Shocked at her shallowness, she'd managed to wangle a seat on a plane to New Zealand. Fortunately Angie had been run off her feet with work, and Iona had flung herself into it, grimly ordering her mind to forget. It hadn't been easy, but she thought she'd coped quite well.

What malevolent fate had brought Luke back into her life again?

At least, she thought just before she dropped back into a restless slumber, unless he had an emergency in the next two days Angie would be dealing with him.

Hours later the tinny, cheerful tattoo of the theme from *Bonanza* woke her. Groaning, she crawled up from beneath the sheets, blinked blearily at the morning and grabbed the work phone. 'Sorted. How can I help you?'

A deep voice said, 'You are not Ms Makepeace.'

Little chills ran down her spine. Her hand tightened on the phone and she had to swallow to ease a suddenly dry throat.

Luke.

No, not Luke. The different names somehow seemed significant. He was not the man she'd made love to in Tahiti. He was Lukas Michelakis, billionaire.

Striving to sound brisk and businesslike, she said, 'Iona Guthrie speaking. I'm afraid Ms Makepeace can't come to the telephone right now. How can I help you?'

'I need someone here, now,' Luke said evenly. 'To take care of a three-year-old girl for the day.'

'What?' Iona literally couldn't believe her ears. Luke Michelakis and a small child simply did not go together.

Impatience tinged his words. 'I am sure you heard correctly.'

Irked by his tone, Iona ignored her whirling thoughts and didn't hesitate. 'Yes. Yes, all right, we can do that.'

'You are sure this person will be reliable and sensible?'

'Yes.'

'I need to leave in half an hour.'

Iona's mouth thinned. 'I'll be there as soon as I can, but I'm not going to be able to make it in that time.'

'*You* will be here?'

She reacted to his incredulous words with chilly aloofness. 'L—Mr Michelakis, I'm a trained kindergarten teacher, and the only person you're likely to get during the weekend at such short notice. The child will be safe in my care.'

'Oh, call me Luke as you did in Tahiti—we know each other well, you and I,' he said derisively.

'So why are you questioning my ability to care for the child?' The moment the words escaped from her mouth she wished she could call them back.

Sure enough Luke said, 'Now you're being deliberately naïve. In Tahiti you were my lover—a very charming and sensuous lover—and nothing more.'

Of course he was right, but his casual statement hurt.

He waited, as if for a comment, and when Iona remained silent he went on brusquely, 'I have no idea what you will be like with children. And if Chloe is not safe in your care you will pay.'

'Are you expecting a kidnap attempt?' Into a taut silence, she said, 'I certainly wouldn't be much use if that's likely to occur.'

'I am *not* expecting a kidnap attempt,' he said coldly.

'I'm relieved. If all you want is a temporary nanny I can do that. I'm capable and competent when it comes to children. And I like them. I also have a current practising certificate which I'll be pleased to show you when I arrive.'

The pause seemed to drag on for ever, but finally he said, 'Very well. It seems I am forced to rely on you for this, so I will expect you here within the half hour. Give me your address. I shall send a car.'

Iona drew in a deep breath, but stifled her intemperate reply when she remembered Angie's delight at the prospect of an uninterrupted day with her sons. 'Thank you,' she snapped.

Angie had said it the night before: this was work, and the business needed the money.

Luke repeated her address after her, then warned, 'Be ready,' and hung up.

As she scurried around, assembling a kit that would keep a three-year-old girl interested, questions raced through Iona's mind. Was little Chloe his daughter? If so, she thought sickly, he must have been married or in a relationship when he'd made love to her in Tahiti.

It should have been a relief to be able to despise him. It certainly explained his antagonism; did he think she'd tell his wife he'd been unfaithful?

Never!

But it seemed unlikely that the mother of his child was with him; if she were, she'd be the one looking after her daughter.

By the time the taxi arrived Iona was ready. She'd had to forego breakfast and a much-needed cup of tea, but her large carry-all had enough in it to keep even a demanding child busy for a day. Stomach clenching, she walked out of the penthouse lift, disconcerted to find Luke in the doorway.

Like a lion lying in wait for an antelope.

Dismayed, Iona ignored the treacherous heat burning along her cheekbones while she replied to his greeting.

A narrowed tawny-gold gaze took in her clothes—cotton trousers that that reached halfway down her calves, a bright T-shirt, sandals. One black brow climbed.

'Practical,' he observed cooly, 'if a little informal.'

'New Zealanders are noted for their informality,' she returned in her most professional tone.

'I recall that very well.'

A lazily sensual note beneath the words raised the tiny hairs on the back of Iona's neck and sent a forbidden, ruthlessly exciting response shivering through her. Damn him, she thought furiously as flashbacks of the time they'd spent together surged back, drugging and potent.

Blurting the first thing that came to her mind, she asked, 'When am I going to meet my charge for the day?'

'Right now,' he said crisply, and reached out.

For a startled moment Iona thought he intended to take her arm.

A primitive, protective reaction twisted her backwards, but his hand closed around the handles of her bag and he said softly, lethally, 'You are quite safe. If you want me to touch you again you will have to ask me to do so.'

Iona stiffened. OK, so until she'd fled Tahiti probably no one had ever turned Luke Michelakis down, but she'd never promised him anything; right from the start they'd both known that what they shared was nothing stronger or more permanent than a holiday romance.

She'd just ended it a little sooner than either had expected.

Which didn't give him any right to be offended.

But then the adored only son of a powerful Greek patriarch would certainly be spoilt. Especially one who looked like some beautiful, vengeful god from ancient times.

And there was the spectre of the child's absent mother...

Choosing to ignore his terse statement, she relinquished the bag to him.

Cynically amused at her care to avoid touching his fingers, Lukas said, 'This way.'

For a moment he'd been going to ask her why she'd left him in Tahiti, but she was now his employee—and he'd overstepped the professional bounds already.

Besides, he had not allowed himself to care. He'd learned young that women were naturally treacherous—a lesson cut into his heart when his father's second wife had engineered his expulsion from the family.

He'd vowed then never to trust another woman, so it would be foolish of him to expect more from Iona.

Aristo Michelakis, his father, had expected his twenty-year-old son to fail, to fall into oblivion. Twelve years later, Lukas allowed himself a swift glance around his opulent surroundings.

He'd been coldly, furiously determined to prove both himself and his innocence of the crime he'd been accused of. That driving need had guided him into a career where his brilliant brain and passion were fully utilised. He had seized his opportunities with a zest that had led to huge success in spite of his father's attempts to ruin him.

And he had his pick of lovers from the women who'd flocked to him, drawn by his fortune and the face he'd inherited from his father.

Always he'd made sure his lovers expected nothing more from him than good sex and his protection as long as the affair lasted.

Then Chloe had been born—another outcast from the family. She'd brought a new dimension to his life, but his attitude to his lovers remained the same.

So why had Iona stuck in his mind?

Because she had been—different. He set Iona's bag beside a chair and glanced down at her, resisting an impulse to run a finger across that unsmiling, infuriatingly desirable mouth. What would she do if he kissed her? His body tightened in swift, fierce response even as he dismissed the thought.

She was not exactly beautiful, but she'd been a passionate and generous lover, and he'd enjoyed their interlude—perhaps a little too much. It irritated him to admit it, but her abrupt departure had angered him. He had missed her.

However, it was ridiculous—a stupid, unnecessary overreaction—to feel she'd betrayed him.

Acutely aware of his swift glance and his silence, Iona was glad to meet the child she was looking after. Chloe was tall for her age, as befitted the daughter of such a tall man, with large dark eyes, and a mouth that subtly echoed that of her father. It quirked in a fleeting smile for him before she transferred a solemn gaze to Iona, who introduced herself calmly.

'Hello. My name is Iona Guthrie, and we'll be spending some time together today while your father has a meeting.'

'He always goes to meetings.'

The statement, although made entirely without rancour, wrung Iona's heart.

'I'm sure he's very busy, but we'll have fun together, you and I.'

Chloe scanned Iona's large bag. 'Are you going to stay 'cos Neelie's gone?'

'Only for today,' Luke told her.

Who was Neelie? Mother? Nanny?

'I've brought some things you might like to do with me, and a few books you might not have seen before,' Iona said.

That seemed to satisfy Chloe, who obeyed immediately when her father announced, 'Take Ms Guthrie out onto the terrace, Chloe, and show her your horse.'

Horse? Surely he didn't carry around a horse as part of his ménage?

He did. A splendid rocking horse, dappled grey, with flared nostrils and flowing mane, and a saddle and bridle fit for a queen. 'His name is Pegasus,' Chloe informed her in that precise, neutral voice.

She glanced up at Iona, who asked, 'And does he fly, like the horse in the legend?'

It seemed she might have passed some subtle test, for the child smiled at her. 'Nearly. He used to be Lukas's horse when he was a little boy.' Her tone expressed a hint of disbelief, as though she simply couldn't conceive of her father ever being small enough to ride the horse.

Why did she call him by his first name?

More to the point, where the heck was her mother? Dead? Divorced? Not interested?

None of your business, Iona warned herself, and said gravely, 'You and your father are very lucky. Pegasus is a magnificent animal.'

'He's my *best* friend.'

Like her father, Chloe spoke excellent English; unlike him she had no trace of an accent. Not, Iona recalled, that Luke had much—really, only the merest hint...

Just enough to imbue every word he said with a subtle under-note of disturbing sensuality that had deepened when they'd made love.

Don't even think about that!

Iona said, 'Pegasus is lucky too—to have such a good friend as you. Would you like to show me how well you can ride him?'

After a moment Chloe hitched up her skirt and climbed onto the horse, setting it rocking with a gleeful enthusiasm that warmed Iona's heart.

'She is reserved, but not shy,' her father said from behind.

Startled, Iona swivelled. Dressed in a superbly tailored business suit that showed off his lean, powerful body, he was a formidable presence. A stab of awareness shocked Iona with its swift intensity, reminding her of all the reasons—those foolish, dangerous reasons— she'd embarked on their affair.

Moving out of earshot of the child, she asked in her most practical voice, 'Is there anything I should know about Chloe before you go?' When his black brows drew together she added briskly, 'I gather her mother is not here? No doubt Chloe will be missing her.'

'You assume too much.'

Iona lifted her head at the touch of hauteur in his words. Something odd was going on here, and if it was likely to affect Chloe she needed to know about it. 'Very well,' she said, in a tone that matched his for bluntness, 'but *is* there anything I should be aware of?'

Lukas didn't try to moderate the frown that always made his subordinates tread very carefully. It didn't seem to affect Iona. Those unusual sea-shaded eyes mirrored both the colour of whatever she wore and her emotions. Today they were a direct, cool blue with a hint of challenge.

Yesterday in the powder room when she'd been half-naked they'd been blue-green, wide and shocked, and then full of mystery.

He'd had to rein in a hunger so elemental and direct it had taken him by surprise.

Why the hell *had* she run away from him in Tahiti? Because he'd cast his suggestion she stay with him as a proposition rather than a proposal?

Surely she'd realised it was too early in their relationship for an admission of anything more than a passionate hunger? He'd wanted them to get to know each other—discover if their superb compatibility extended beyond the raptures of the bed—but clearly she hadn't reciprocated those inchoate, hardly formed feelings.

Ruthlessly repressing the sharp twist of sensation in his gut at the memory of just how good they'd been together, he forced his mind back to her question.

Discreet she might be, but he wasn't going to let her in on any family secrets. He'd had enough of seeing his private life—or fiction about it—splashed across newsprint. If the circumstances of Chloe's birth and his subsequent adoption of the child ever leaked out, some parts of the media would have a field day.

That he could cope with. What made it imperative that he keep the secret until he could trust Iona was his father's latest threat—to contest the adoption and demand custody of the daughter Aristo had refused to accept.

CHAPTER THREE

STILL, Lukas reluctantly conceded Iona had a point.

Yesterday he'd ordered his security people to check her and her cousin out; the report had arrived first thing that morning. They were clean—practically saints, he thought sardonically.

After a glance at Chloe's absorbed little face as she rocked rhythmically on the horse, Luke made up his mind, but even so, he chose his words with care.

'Her mother has never been part of Chloe's life.' She hadn't even named her. He'd called her Chloe after his maternal grandmother.

Irritated, because the silken allure of Iona's skin and the grace of her movements still had the power to stir him, he went on more curtly than he'd intended, 'I have always cared for her, and her nanny has been with her since she was a year old. Unfortunately she was called away to England last night, so it is possible Chloe will talk about Neelie. I have explained the circumstances to her—that Neelie had to go to her sick mother—and she appears to understand and accept that. I have left a contact number beside the telephone; if there is any emergency—but *only* in an emergency—ring me.'

Her eyes veiled by her lashes, Iona nodded and replied with composure, 'I don't panic easily.'

Lukas resisted another flash of hunger, deep and arousing. She didn't fit the classical standards of beauty—her face was striking rather than pretty—but something about it and her smoothly lissome body still retained a disturbing power to intrigue him.

However, he had responsibilities he couldn't neglect, and although it was some months since he'd last had a woman it would be inconvenient to embark—*re-embark*, he corrected cynically—on an affair right now with a woman who'd already caused him enough sleepless nights.

And if he'd learned anything in his life it was to control the urges of his body.

Iona resolutely turned her face away to watch Chloe, absorbed on her flying steed. Luke should mean nothing to her, and neither should the possibility that he'd been married when he'd made love to her with such blazing desire.

Yet she struggled with a foolish sense of betrayal.

Ignoring it, she asked, 'Roughly what time are you planning to be back?'

'This meeting should finish at a reasonable time— before five o'clock,' he told her, a note of austerity in his words telling her he wasn't used to being questioned. 'If it threatens to stretch further I—or my PA—will contact you. Do you have an appointment tonight?'

Iona met eyes that were unexpectedly keen. 'No.'

His expression didn't change as he turned and called, 'Chloe, I have to go now.'

The child scrambled down from the rocking horse and came running with outstretched arms. Watching him swoop down to lift her high, Iona relaxed. Luke wasn't effusive, but his love for his daughter was clear; he held her with great tenderness, and murmured something in a language Iona supposed to be Greek.

Forget the way that voice sends shivers down your spine, she warned herself. Concentrate on Chloe.

Nothing to worry about there—the child's body language proclaimed her complete faith and trust in her father. Nestled against his big frame, she looked tiny as she gave him his kiss with perfect confidence, and his hard-hewn, handsome face softened.

Somehow that touched a nerve in Iona.

Gently he put Chloe down and straightened up. 'So, be good for Miss Iona while I'm gone.' He looked at Iona. 'I have ordered a snack to arrive at ten for both of you, and lunch will be brought up at midday. Chloe has a nap after lunch for half an hour, and then a drink and some fruit when she wakes.'

'Lukas, can Miss Iona take me for a swim when I wake up?'

Smiling down at her, he replied, 'No, because she will not have brought anything to wear in the water.'

His daughter pouted, but didn't push her luck. Obviously Luke's decisions were non-negotiable.

Iona said, 'Actually, I noticed the pool yesterday so I brought my togs.' She looked at him directly, aware of a swift streak of colour along her cheekbones. In Tahiti she'd swum naked, and from the gleam beneath his lashes she suspected he was remembering. 'I have a lifesaving certificate.'

For an intimidating moment he was silent before his mouth curved in an oblique smile. 'I know you are an excellent swimmer. I see no reason why you shouldn't swim together,' he conceded to a beaming Chloe, adding, 'But only if you promise me that when Miss Iona tells you it is time to get out you do not plead to stay in for just a few minutes longer.'

Chloe's face wrinkled in earnestness. 'I won't, Lukas. I will be as good as gold, like Neelie says.'

He looked amused, but spoke directly to Iona. 'Chloe is an excellent swimmer for her age, but too much time in the water turns her lips blue and makes her shiver.'

During the morning the child's artless frankness built a picture for Iona of a man who could be stern but wasn't unfair, and whose arms held all Chloe wanted. She referred to the nanny with affection, but clearly it was her father who was the sum and substance of her life.

The situation nagged at Iona. Perhaps he hadn't known about the child when they'd had that fling in Tahiti?

But he'd said her mother had never figured in Chloe's life.

Apart from bearing her and giving birth, Iona thought ironically. Whatever, she told herself severely as she tucked the child into bed for her afternoon nap, it was absolutely *none* of her business.

While Chloe slept Iona sat out on the terrace with the book she'd been reading for the past few days, exasperated when it no longer held her attention. She got up and walked over to the edge of the terrace and leant against the railing.

Up above, the glinting waters of the harbour clouds marched in ranks across a radiant sky. After Gavin had drowned she hadn't been able to bear even looking at the sea; she'd deliberately chosen Tahiti for her holiday because the island location made it impossible for her to avoid the ocean. She'd forced herself to accept and overcome her fear.

It had worked, although not in the way she hoped. The bleak sense of responsibility for Gavin's death had been overwhelmed by the haze of sensuality Luke had woven around her—a sensuality she'd welcomed, enjoyed, basked in...

Driven by restlessness, she turned away and paced around across the terrace. Whoever had designed this garden had created a rooftop paradise, its almost tropical lushness forming a background to a carefully tended magnolia that held breathtaking, opulently rosy goblets up to the sky.

Idly, she bent to sniff a gardenia flower, wondering what it would be like to be truly rich, one of those people whose deep pockets meant that money was the least of their concerns.

People about as far removed as they could be from Angie, who had three full-time workers to worry about as well as her children, and the ever-present burden of the debts her ex-husband had left behind when he'd skipped out of the country.

Angie had admitted last night that things were tough. How tough? Was she secretly hoping Iona might return to her previous career as a nursery teacher?

If so, surely she'd have said something?

Probably not. She and Angie had no other relatives but each other. Angie could be keeping her on from some sense of family duty.

Entirely *unnecessary* family duty! Iona made up her mind; she'd ask Angie directly, because she could always find a job in a nursery school or a daycare centre. It wouldn't pay as well as working for Angie, but she'd manage.

Earlier she'd read Chloe one of the books she'd packed, delighted when the story sparked the child's imagination. They'd acted it out, with Chloe suggesting embellishments, some outrageous, some affecting—like her suggestion that a baby brother be incorporated so the heroine would have someone to play with.

'Would you like to keep that book for yourself?' Iona had surprised herself by asking at lunchtime, when she'd noted that Chloe was reluctant to put the book down.

Chloe's eyes widened. 'Oh, yes,' she breathed, adding conscientiously, 'Yes, please, Miss Iona.' She held it out. 'Can you write in it?'

Touched, Iona said, 'Of course I can.' She fished out her pen and printed on the title page: *'For Chloe, so she remembers a lovely day in Auckland. From Iona.'*

But Chloe frowned when Iona read out the dedication. 'You have to say *'With love from,'*' she said.

Iona's heart stilled a precarious second, then began to beat again. It would be very easy to become fond of this child.

She said, 'Goodness, how could I have forgotten?' And inscribed the extra words in the right place.

Chloe beamed. 'I will be careful of it,' she promised earnestly.

The book had gone to bed with her after another reading. Now, thinking of the pleasure the simple gift had given the child, Iona smiled, then turned as a voice from behind interrupted her thoughts.

'I'm awake.'

And ready for the swim she'd been promised.

Chloe's nanny had brought her up to be self-sufficient; she was already wearing a cute little two-piece, almost covered by a towel draped around her shoulders. A bright yellow cap dangled from one small hand.

Hiding a smile, Iona organised them both into the pool, relaxing a little when she discovered the child was like a small eel in the water. They splashed and played together until a cry of 'Lukas!' from Chloe whipped Iona's head around.

Luke was striding through the glass doors and into the pool enclosure, tall and extremely sophisticated in that killer suit, the sun gleaming blue-black on his arrogantly poised head.

Iona's spine melted and sharp darts of sensation shot through her. She knew what it was—desire, sweet and treacherous, hauntingly familiar...

Yet different now, deeper and more potent than the purely sensuous sensations he'd previously aroused. Somehow Luke's obvious love for the child swimming at top speed towards him had worked a change in Iona's response to him.

A *dangerous* change, she thought, nerves quivering as she stood up, only to sink back into the water. Her sleek one-piece clung to her like a second skin, tempting her to duck beneath the surface in a stupid, childish reflex.

Luke had seen her naked so often any novelty value had to be long gone, but she was relieved he wasn't looking her way; in fact, she might just as well not have been there. His whole attention was focused on Chloe, and the smile he gave when he pulled his clamorous daughter out of the pool did something very odd to Iona's heart.

He said something that lit up the little girl's face then smiled and wrapped her wet body in the towel like a small, wriggly mummy before hugging her.

Only after he'd kissed her forehead did he look over her sleek black head towards Iona. Acutely and foolishly self-conscious, she stood again, feeling the water stream from her.

'There is a problem,' he told her, eyes on her face. Without waiting for an answer he said, 'This meeting might not finish until late tonight. So you will stay until I come back.'

It was not a request.

'Very well,' Iona said, irked by his cool assumption that her time was his to command.

He set Chloe down and commanded, 'Run off and get back into your clothes. I wish to talk to Miss Iona.'

Chloe raced off, obviously eager not to miss a single precious moment of his presence.

Luke said abruptly, 'I presume your cousin can bring you clothes for an overnight stay.'

'No, she's busy today.' And when she did get back home with her two tired boys Angie certainly wouldn't want to be forced to collect clothes from across the city.

Eyes slightly narrowed, he said, 'In that case I can organise for someone on my staff to fetch them.'

The thought of some unknown person going through her clothes revolted her. 'No,' she said definitely, and hauled herself out of the water to give herself time to collect her wits.

And also because for some reason she found it demeaning to be at his feet—below his feet in fact, so that he stood looking down at her like some medieval despot with authority over life and death.

Or the power to take whatever woman he desired.

Somewhere deep inside Iona those long-repressed sensations stirred again, tantalising and decadent.

Frowning, he agreed, 'I suppose not. So what do you suggest?'

Reminding herself of Angie's shaky financial situation, Iona bit back impetuous words. 'I've brought a change of clothes,' she told him. His brows lifted and she said wryly, 'It's a sensible precaution if you're look-ing after children.' And her underclothes would dry overnight.

He nodded. 'Toothbrush? Toothpaste?'

'I'll use salt.' And when he looked startled she added, 'Or baking soda. It tastes vile but it does the job.'

His mouth twitched. 'It sounds appalling, but for-tunately there is no need for you to suffer. I've already organised with the concierge for you to order what you want.'

The slight shrug of her shoulders reminded her she was barefoot and revealing far too much wet skin. Her hair hung in sopping confusion around her face, and water dripped off the end of her nose.

So? she thought defiantly. She didn't—*couldn't*—care what Luke was thinking while he watched her with burnished intent eyes, as opaque as gold.

'Thank you,' she said. 'I'll go and change.'

She turned away, only to be stopped in mid-stride by his crisp command. 'A moment. Stay very still.'

Iona froze, aware of the tickling of some insect on her shoulder. 'It is only a bee,' Luke said, and flicked it off, then smoothed over her skin.

The brush of his fingers sent swift needles of pleasure through her before he pulled his hand away, leaving her oddly bereft.

She didn't dare look at him, and no words would come past the lump in her throat until she'd stepped away and picked up her towel, wrapping it around her waist as though it were armour. 'Poor thing. It must have fallen into the pool.'

'Possibly. Or perhaps it thought you were another flower.'

A faint trace of cynicism in his tone made her bold enough to say, 'In that case it's got a very poor future, I'm afraid. I hope it didn't go back into the water.'

His voice sounded cool and faintly speculative when he said, 'It flew into one of the trees. You worry about a bee?'

'They sound like summer. And I like honey. Thank you.'

His expression was unreadable. 'It was nothing. Tonight you will sleep in the bedroom next to Chloe's. She goes to bed at six-thirty, and usually sleeps without waking until about the same time the next morning.'

'She sounds the perfect child,' Iona said lightly, and headed towards the little pavilion where they'd left their towels and a change of clothes. She felt shaky and light-headed, as though she'd been secretly starving for Luke's touch, missing some essential part of her life without even realising it.

She had to get a grip. The pavilion beckoned like a small haven. She was almost there when Chloe came dashing out, her clothes pulled on anyhow. If Iona had been the child's nanny she'd have caught and tidied her, but that could wait.

And so, she thought as she closed the door behind her, could Luke Michelakis.

When she emerged, fully dressed and a little more composed, father and daughter had gone inside. After a moment's hesitation she followed the sound of voices to Chloe's room; she hovered before the door, repressing a start when it opened unexpectedly.

'Chloe's in the shower,' her father said. 'She was shivering so I thought it wise. Come, I'll show you your room.'

He strode past her and opened the door, standing

aside so that she could see into the room. During her inspection of the penthouse she'd wondered who would sleep here. Clearly Chloe's nanny shared the lifestyle of her employer.

She said, 'It's charming, thank you.'

'I have to thank *you*,' he said unexpectedly. 'I am extremely grateful to you for staying with Chloe.'

How could a smile melt bones? It was totally unfair; Luke did not need his enormous wealth and position to win his reputation as a playboy. When he turned on the charm he was knee-weakeningly magnetic.

And seeing him with his daughter had added an extra depth to that stunning, sexy smile.

This is *business*, Iona thought bracingly, and so was that smile—a deliberate attempt to win her over. 'It's my job.'

'I didn't expect the discussions I'm involved in to last as long as they are, but politicians and their advisors cannot be hurried.' Wide shoulders lifted in an unapologetic Mediterranean shrug. 'Meals have been organised for you both. If you need anything at all, ask the concierge.' He turned, then stopped to say, 'I always ring Chloe to say goodnight to her, so expect a call soon after six.'

Arrogant he certainly was, but no one could doubt his love for his daughter. Iona's heart expanded. 'When I go to bed I'll leave our doors open so I can hear her if she wakes.'

'Thank you. There should be a baby monitor,' he said, his tone tinged with exasperation. 'I assume Neelie forgot to unpack it before she left. However, Chloe doesn't wake at night unless she's ill. And if that happens I wish to be told immediately.'

Iona nodded. 'As well as being a nursery school

teacher, I've had quite a bit of experience babysitting my cousin's children, so I have a fairly good idea of the difference between just a sore tummy and something more serious.'

He smiled again, and Iona felt a languorous appreciation shimmer through every nerve in her body. 'How very fortunate I am to rediscover you,' he said softly.

Struggling to resist that compelling charm, Iona said coolly, 'Good luck can come to the most unlikely people.'

Although Luke's lashes drooped, his expression remained controlled. 'Indeed it can. And a sensible person will always be grateful for what the gods offer without expecting any further favours.' Switching subjects, he finished, 'I hope to be back before midnight, but feel free to go to bed whenever you wish.'

'I shall,' she said sweetly, relieved to hear Chloe call from the bedroom. 'I'll go to her,' she told him. 'I'm sure you want to get away.'

Ignoring her, he strode back into his daughter's room. After a moment's hesitation Iona followed. He stooped to drop a kiss on his flushed, towel-draped daughter, tickled her until she collapsed into giggles, then gathered her hands in one of his own and pressed a kiss into one palm before straightening. Tall and commanding as he was, the combination of leashed male strength and tenderness touched Iona's newly vulnerable heart.

Careful, she thought warily. This was a very temporary situation—Luke and Chloe would be gone within days and she'd be stupid to let herself become emotionally involved with either the man or his child.

To Chloe he said, 'Soon we'll be staying on the island

and I shall not go to a meeting for at least seven sleeps. How does that sound?'

Judging by the radiance of her beam he'd offered his daughter a taste of paradise. Iona felt like an intruder in this picture of domestic felicity.

Innocently the child asked, 'Can Miss Iona come too?'

'Miss Iona is too busy here to take a holiday with us,' Luke said smoothly, his gaze cool and dismissive as it travelled to Iona. 'Besides, Neelie should be back by then.'

Well, that relegated her to her proper place, Iona thought on a foolish spurt of defiance. Substitute nurse-maid—yet she'd loved being a nursery school teacher, so why should his words sting?

Because she was so stupidly, *violently* aware of him?

Iona followed Luke out into the hall, watching with some bemusement while he fitted a nightlight into an electric socket there. He kept startling her with small actions that seemed at odds with his intimidating character, but then, his daughter was clearly his Achilles' heel.

Iona was smiling slightly at the Greek reference when he stood up. Lord, but he was *big*, she thought involuntarily. Big in every sense of the word—tall, broad-shouldered, lithely elegant, and with a presence that filled the place.

He turned and caught her watching him. Iona's heart gave a nervous leap in her chest and a traitorous antici-pation stabbed her with sweet heat.

The smoky gleam in his eyes was banished by a will far stronger than hers. Coolly he said, 'If she wakes she likes to see a glow outside. We do a lot of travelling, and I think it helps her orient herself in a new place.'

'I'll make sure it's left on when she goes to bed,' Iona promised in her most professional tone.

Luke had barely gone when Angie rang. 'How are things going?' she enquired.

'Fine,' Iona said automatically.

'Do you think your gorgeous alpha boss would approve of us—you and me—taking the little girl to the zoo tomorrow? It's Children's Day, and the forecast is for gorgeous weather; I've promised the boys we'll check out the tiger babies and penguins.'

'I doubt if he'll say yes, but no harm in trying,' Iona told her.

To be fair, a man with his position and power had reason to be cautious about his daughter's security. Not in New Zealand, she thought, then frowned, because even New Zealand wasn't necessarily safe.

Half an hour after Iona had put her cell phone down there was call from the concierge. 'I have a parcel here for you,' he said. 'I'll send it up with a porter.'

It came from a very exclusive shop, one that specialised in overseas labels, and was addressed to her.

Tense for no reason, Iona let Chloe open the bag. Inside, tenderly tucked into a sheet of pastel tissue paper, was a garment in a soft rose-beige that turned out to be a nightgown.

So Luke had ignored her—just gone ahead and organised this. Warily Iona eyed another smaller parcel in the bag.

'Are you going to open that one too?' Chloe asked eagerly when she made no attempt to do so.

'You can if you like.'

Very carefully Chloe peeled back the seal and folded the paper away, first the wrapping, then the tissue beneath. Colour surged into Iona's skin. As well as the exquisite nightgown Luke had bought her a bra and a pair of panties, lace-trimmed scraps of frivolity that deepened the blush on her cheeks.

A swift glance showed her that he'd judged her size perfectly. Iona bit her lip, feeling obscurely as though she'd been bought.

'Oh, here's a toothbrush,' she said with relief. 'And some toothpaste.' With them were soap and moisturiser, cosmetics so expensive she suspected they'd cost more than her week's salary.

Her stomach contracted. Of course she wouldn't use them. Well, the toothpaste and brush would be fine, but the others smacked of some sort of pay-off.

For Tahiti? Surely not?

Of *course* not, she told herself robustly. That would be nastily petty, and the Luke she'd known wasn't petty. OK, so she'd left him in Tahiti with no explanation, nothing more than the briefest of notes, and he'd probably been astonished—possibly even angry—but they had made no promises to each other, and there were plenty of women eager to warm his bed.

While she'd been his lover she'd met several of those women.

She looked down at the exquisite fripperies. It was silly to take the contents personally; Luke was a very rich man, accustomed to giving orders. He'd probably commanded some minion to buy and despatch these pretty things. As for getting the size right—well, he was the sort of man who noticed things.

After dinner Chloe went off to bed without protest,

asking only that Iona read the book again, and then innocently holding her face up to be kissed before she was tucked in.

Much later Iona checked her soundly sleeping charge. For a few seconds she stood beside Chloe's bed, picking out her resemblance to her father, and wondering where the little girl had been when her father had holidayed in Tahiti eighteen months ago.

Like so many questions, it would never be answered, but the knowledge of the child's existence tarnished the memory of those days and nights.

She turned and went out, careful to leave the door open. And, although her bed was huge and supremely comfortable, she lay awake for what seemed a long time before dropping off.

Much later she woke with a start. Lifting herself on one elbow, she strained to hear. Nothing…no sound but the hum of distant traffic…yet something had alerted her. Chloe?

She climbed stealthily out of bed and grabbed her T-shirt and the towel she'd put close by in case her charge woke. Ears straining, she listened again, but whatever had woken her was silent. Perhaps Chloe had murmured in her sleep…

After shrugging into the shirt she peeked warily past her door. Nothing moved in the dim glow of the night-light. And then her stomach clenched when she thought she heard a sound from the child's room.

Luke. Of course it had to be him. But she needed to be sure.

She wrapped the towel around her waist, then tiptoed through the door. And stopped abruptly at the sight of the dark form standing beside the child's bed.

Intensely relieved, she recognised Luke immediately

and shot back out. She didn't hear him move, but he caught up to her before she got to her own bedroom door.

'I am sorry to have disturbed you,' he said in a voice pitched to carry to her ears only.

He'd taken off his tie and coat; in the soft yellow glow of the nightlight the fine fabric of his white shirt contrasted starkly with sleek olive skin, showing off the clean, athletic lines of his powerful body.

Inside Iona a treacherous need smouldered back into life, a forbidden, tantalising expectancy she remembered only too well. She swallowed. 'I heard something,' she said in explanation, then stopped and swallowed again because her voice sounded oddly breathless.

And she must seem a total idiot, coming out with such an obvious statement.

He nodded, eyes glinting, mouth curving in a smile that shook her defences. 'You heard me trying not to be heard.'

Quick heat burned through her. The soft T-shirt fabric felt like sacking against her acutely sensitive skin. Her breath locked in her lungs when his gaze fell to her breasts.

To her intense relief a sound from Chloe's room froze them both.

He said quietly, 'She's just turning over.'

Trying desperately to control her chaotic reactions, Iona waited until the child settled into silence again, then pushed open her own door.

Poised for flight into the refuge of her room, she said over her shoulder, 'She went to bed without any problems.'

'Good. You got the parcel?'

Thank heavens the dim nightlight couldn't reveal her scalding cheeks. She said stiffly, 'Yes. Thank you.'

'You didn't like the gown?'

CHAPTER FOUR

DAMN him, why couldn't he pretend he hadn't noticed? Tiny shivers of sensation scudded the length of Iona's spine, tightening her nerves, shortening her breath, so that her voice sounded strained when she answered, 'It's lovely, but of course I can't accept it.'

'Why not?'

'It's not—' she searched for the right word, finally settling on '—suitable.'

'I'm sorry. I must inform my personal assistant that he's losing his touch.'

The note of amusement in his tone shafted through her. She dragged enough breath into her lungs to say coolly, 'Don't do that—he has great taste.' And, rallying her thoughts into some sort of order, she added, 'I hope your meeting went well. If Chloe wakes again I'll deal with it. Goodnight.'

His assessing gaze didn't waver. 'You must be a very light sleeper—I was as quiet as I could be when I came in. But perhaps you weren't sleeping...?'

A slight uplift of tone at the end of the sentence turned it into a question. No, she realised with a jolt of outrage, *not* a question; he actually wondered if she'd been lying in wait for him.

What conceit! Yet she had to fight back a craven

desire to—what? Surrender? He seemed entirely relaxed, but she could sense a humming energy about him, a slow, fierce lick of fire that called to something deeply subversive in her.

She didn't dare speak in case her voice gave her away. He must have taken her silence for assent because she felt his hand on her shoulder, light yet somehow possessive. His touch sent shivers of anticipation coursing through her, zinging through nerves and cells like heat lightning, dazzling and dangerous and powerful.

Her mind screamed *Get the hell out of here*, but a more primal urgency consumed her, keeping her still and acquiescent as he turned her.

His eyes glittered and his voice was rough and deep. 'Perhaps you were thinking—as I have been all day— that we should not ungratefully ignore this gift of time from the gods.'

His hand slid to her back, the other lifting her chin. Excitement hammered through her. The subdued light emphasised the arrogant perfection of his features, the sensuous mouth and intent, elemental hunger in his lion eyes.

'Tell me you forgot me,' he ordered, his voice harsh.

Yes, tell him, caution insisted. Lie to him…

'No.' The admission came out like a sigh, softly languorous, silken with need and longing.

At last, she thought with a relief so intense it blocked out everything but delight. *At last.*

She had been waiting for this ever since—ever since she'd looked at the mirror in the penthouse powder room and seen him standing in the doorway. Without realising it she'd been waiting for his arms to close around her and pull her against him, for his lips to touch hers in a deliciously provocative butterfly kiss on the corner of her mouth.

Waiting for the driving beat of his heart into hers, the subtle arousal of his body, the powerful seduction of being protected and desired at the same time…

Waiting for Luke.

And for the sweet, powerful hunger that leapt into life in every cell of her body, filling her with the passion only he could rouse in her.

The shock of realisation sent a rush of sensation through her, tightening her breasts and heating the pit of her stomach. For a few stunned seconds she stayed immobile, until the reality of everything hit her in an elemental, all-consuming flood, weakening her knees so that she swayed into him.

He understood the silent surrender, bending his head so that she felt the soft whisper of his words against her sensitised lips. 'Good. Because I could not forget you.'

It was like falling into an inferno, a headlong surrender to passion so intense and incandescent the primal, white-hot honesty of desire burned away common sense and caution and the cold chill of reality.

At first his lips were controlled and seeking, but the wildfire intensity of her response must have set fire to him too, because his mouth hardened and the kiss became an act of total possession, deepening into a hunger so blatant it demanded everything from her.

Iona shuddered at the exquisite sensations his touch awakened in her, and his arms tightened, bringing her into intimate juxtaposition with his hard loins. An instant rush of adrenalin stimulated her into complete arousal, recklessly whetting her appetite for him into a sensual clamour that made nonsense of all her forebodings.

She wanted him with a desperate vulnerability that terrified her, jolting her into awareness of what she was doing—what he was offering…

Gasping, she jerked her head back, rejecting the carnal impulses that rioted through every cell and clouded her mind in a haze of heady, dangerous desire.

He loosened his grip, but didn't let her go. 'So, it is still there,' he said softly. 'What is it, do you think, this incredible urge to carry you off somewhere and never let you out of my bed again?'

Iona moistened her tender lips, an effort of will almost negated when his kindling gaze followed the tiny movement of her tongue.

For a pathetic second she wondered if his comment meant he might feel something more than naked, unsatisfied lust, but he wasn't wanting her in his life, only in his bed.

'Sex,' she croaked, brutally honest. Sex for him—but so much more than that for her.

He laughed. 'Then what are we going to do about it?' he said, and bent his head again.

Iona stiffened, fighting the passionate need that roared back into life. 'I'll bite you,' she threatened.

But the words came out low and husky, intimate and too languorous to impress him. He kissed the pulse that beat wildly in her throat, his lips lingering with erotic effect against the soft skin, so that Iona shivered again, desperately resisting the tempting whisper to surrender, let him take her, lose herself again in the voluptuous enchantment of his lovemaking.

'I remember your bites,' he growled, and gently nipped the sensitive pleasure point where her neck met her shoulders. 'I soon learned that like the tigress, once you used your teeth on me your completion would soon come.'

'You were wrong,' she managed, and put paid to every instinct by pulling back, away from the taut magnetism of his body, of the mindless sex he was offering.

Been there, done that, thrown away the T-shirt, she thought wildly as she fought to repress the smouldering pangs of addictive hunger, so close to craving it almost broke through the tattered remnants of her common sense.

'If I am wrong, why are you trembling?'

She shook her head and pushed against the door. It didn't give, and she couldn't think how to open it, until Luke said something in Greek and turned the handle, pushing it back.

'Go now,' he ordered, the words low and harsh from between almost clenched teeth. 'Before I take up the offer your body is making. You want me every bit as much as I want you—at least admit that.'

Indignation at her own weakness lifted her chin, froze her voice. 'Goodnight.'

Swiftly she slipped through the door and closed it firmly on him, furious at her white-hot reaction to his potent, untrammelled masculinity. Halfway to the bed she had to stop for a few seconds and consciously relax her strained muscles, fight back a hunger that had never gone away.

Shivering, she crawled under the covers. Although she'd left Tahiti convinced she'd get over him, it had taken only one look from him to make her realise his power over her. But until that kiss of a few minutes ago she hadn't accepted that the feelings she'd stringently repressed were too potent to ignore.

Since Tahiti she hadn't been able to summon even

a flicker of interest in any other man. So why hadn't she realised that Luke had altered her in a fundamental way?

He hadn't changed. Oh, he still wanted her, but for her that was no longer enough.

A pang of deep, painful emotion tore through her.

How likely was it that he had stayed celibate? He was only too cynically aware of the charisma of his smile, the intoxicating, dangerous physical presence that backed up his formidable character. Without a cent to his name he'd still be inundated by panting women.

She'd recognised that dark male authority instantly. The impact of his personality—and the heat of his appreciative metallic survey—had overwhelmed her, melting the ice that had kept her heart and body in a frozen limbo.

Oh, stop it right now, she commanded her treacherous brain in disgust.

Go to sleep.

Easier to say that than do it, she thought wryly when she woke the next morning, eyes heavy with too little rest. Not that sleep had helped; she was still tense and wary—and oddly, *stupidly*, expectant.

The silence probably meant Chloe hadn't woken before her, thank heavens. A glance at her watch elicited a soft gasp. She'd slept through her alarm. She scrambled out of bed, showered, and got into yesterday's clothes, grimacing a little at the dampness of the underwear she'd washed the night before.

Moving quietly, she walked out of her room.

'Good morning.'

With a shocked squeak she jumped. Luke must have prowled up behind her like some predator on the hunt;

she hadn't heard a thing. She took in a jagged breath and turned, catching a black-browed frown.

'You are not afraid of me?' he demanded incredulously.

'Of course not,' she defended herself in her crispest voice.

'Something frightened you?'

She said, 'I thought everyone else was asleep.' It was a pretty lame excuse, and she didn't blame him for the ironic lift of his brows.

'You are of a nervous disposition? I don't remember that.' The words hung for a few seconds, before he said smoothly, 'Surely it is a disadvantage in someone trained to work with children?'

Admitting he was the only person who affected her so intensely was not an option. Matching his raised brows with her own, she ignored his goading tone. 'I'm not nervous—I just didn't expect to have someone come up behind me. Where is Chloe?'

'She is asleep,' he told her. 'Her body is still adjusting to the change in time zones. She will wake up when she is ready. Come and have breakfast—I have a proposition to put to you.'

A pang of shaming anticipation sizzled through her. They were almost the same words he'd used in Tahiti.

Barricades crashing into place, Iona sent him a suspicious glance. He met it with an inscrutable face and cool, dismissive eyes. Clearly the kiss they'd exchanged had had little effect on him.

Chagrined, she chided herself for overreacting so foolishly. But her tone was stiff and cautious when she asked, 'About what?'

'I spoke to Neelie—Chloe's nanny—during the night,' he said calmly. 'The news about her mother is not good, and she will have to stay in England for some time—weeks certainly, months possibly. I have more business meetings for the next couple of days, so I need someone to look after Chloe. I am offering you the job until I leave New Zealand—in about a week. Chloe is clearly enjoying your company, and you seem to have formed a bond with her.'

'I can't,' she said, automatically shaking her head. 'It's not—'

He broke in. 'I have already spoken to your cousin, who tells me she can spare you.'

'How did you contact her?' she demanded, before she could stop herself. 'I have her work phone.'

'I got someone to find her personal phone number,' he said calmly.

When Iona was angry, Lukas noted with wry amusement, her eyes frosted into a cold clear green.

Memories stirred his body into action. Hair like a waterfall against him, the long, silky strands cool and tactile, and skin as sweet and glowing as a white peach...

Yet always, no matter how passionate her surrender, there was a reserve he couldn't penetrate. Emotional closeness had never been on the cards with his previous lovers, yet from his first meeting with Iona he'd found himself challenged by her aloofness—a challenge he should have ignored.

He should certainly have been strong enough last night to resist the temptation to kiss her. Without even trying she was a threat to the foundation on which he'd built his adult life. He enjoyed women but trusted no one; bitter experience had taught him that love didn't last. He was a quick learner, and didn't need more than one lesson.

Nothing like that kiss would happen again, he promised himself. From now on he was determined to keep the situation on a professional level.

Ruthlessly he forced his mind back to the subject in hand. 'Your cousin is happy for you to do this for as long as Chloe needs you.'

The businesslike Ms Makepeace had also shown herself to be a good negotiator in organising Iona's wages and conditions.

He stated them now, watching her face closely. That steely reserve was very evident as she listened, and he couldn't help admiring her gritty dignity when she replied.

'All right.' Her tone was remote and unemotional. 'I agree.'

'You'll want to collect clothes and make arrangements. You can do that while Chloe and I go to the zoo with your cousin and her sons. I've organised a driver for you.'

Her sensuous mouth fell open, was hastily closed, and she lowered thick lashes—a second too late to conceal her surprise. Lukas realised he was enjoying himself. He might regret that kiss—because it was unprofessional—but Iona never bored him.

Did she have a lover, perhaps, waiting impatiently for her? None had shown up in her security check, so almost certainly not. Why? Surely she wasn't still holding the memory of the dead fiancé close to her heart?

Surprised and irritated by the visceral flash of possessiveness his thoughts aroused, he shrugged them off. Her fiancé had died saving her; naturally she would remember him lovingly.

Their Tahitian affair had been a magical experience,

but Chloe was more important to him than any other woman; she needed him as no one else ever had.

Even though Iona made his body sing in a way it never had with any other woman.

'That's very thoughtful of you,' she said then, in a level, aloof voice only a degree or so warmer than ice.

She was still exasperated when she arrived back at the apartment building after scrabbling together a collection of clothes and necessities. Just before she'd closed the door behind her, she had gathered up the references she'd been given when she'd left the nursery school to join Angie.

If Luke wanted proof she'd been a good teacher, she'd take great delight in waving them in his arrogantly handsome face.

The concierge hurried across the foyer to say, 'If you leave your pack and bag here I'll see they get up to the penthouse. Mr Michelakis requested that you meet him at the zoo by the elephant house.' He glanced at his watch. 'In ten minutes,' he said urgently.

Incredulously Iona said, 'Ten minutes?'

'A car is waiting for you,' he said with a little shooing motion of his hand.

Luke was autocratic—so what? It didn't need to affect her. Working for Angie had taught her to cope with everything that came her way.

Not only could she organise a party that would make the social pages for all the right reasons, but she'd turned down propositions—even insulting ones—without once losing her equanimity. She could smile with real amusement at attempts to put her in her place, and control her temper no matter what the provocation.

So why did she feel like exploding at one man's calm assumption that her life was his to organise?

Because he kissed you senseless, and you're scared.

She used the ten minutes in the car to talk herself into composure—a composure that evaporated the moment she caught sight of the small group waiting by the elephant quarters. It was impossible not to notice the way women in the vicinity looked at Luke—with a kind of delighted appreciation as though he fulfilled a set of unspoken, unrecognised conditions.

It was the whole package, Iona thought, her heart contracting; he wore his superbly cut casual clothes with a negligent grace that proclaimed a lithe, toe-curling masculinity and the kind of assets that figured in the financial pages.

That effortless impact was reinforced by the way he towered over most of the people there, with an air of authentic authority and a face like something out of a feverish female fantasy.

But what brought sympathetic smiles—and stirred a dangerous meltdown in Iona's heart—was the way he carried his daughter, as though she was the most precious thing in the universe.

Watching the curve of that dangerously compelling mouth when he set Chloe on her feet, Iona couldn't control her half-apprehensive excitement. Tossed this way and that by dynamic, perilous emotions she wasn't ready to acknowledge, she slowed down.

Luke turned his head. His eyes darkened, and he took Chloe's hand as he straightened to watch Iona come towards them, his face stern.

An apprehensive delight filled her. More perilous than desire, more disturbing than her memories, she tried to tamp it down. Luke Michelakis had no *right* to affect her like this. Losing her heart to him would be—stupid. And terrifying. And forbidden.

After all, what did she know of him apart from his prowess between the sheets?

Only what Angie had told her. And that he loved his daughter.

Don't forget he can be tender and generous when he's making love, some treacherous part of her mind reminded her.

It just wasn't enough to cover the risk, she thought desperately as she came up to them.

Hiding her emotions with a light tone and a smile, she said, 'Hello, kids. Having fun?'

Fortunately both Chloe and the boys greeted her with enthusiasm, each wanting to be the one to tell her a lion had roared at them through the huge glass window that separated the lords of the savannah from fascinated onlookers.

Above the babble of noise Angie grinned at her, but Luke's eyes were cool and measuring when she looked at him.

'All well?' he asked.

'Yes, thank you.'

Once they set off to explore more of the zoo, Iona was surprised when Chloe alternated between her and Luke. Not surprising was the way the boys also gravitated to him, unconsciously awarding him respect and attention. In turn, he was superb with them, calmly curbing their high spirits, and treating them with the same interested courtesy with which he spoke to Chloe.

Iona didn't dare glance Angie's way. Until now she'd thought the boys were getting over their father's abandonment, but the uncomplicated hero-worship in two pairs of eyes revealed just how much they missed a male presence in their lives.

On the way back to the apartment Luke lifted his gaze from his daughter's head, cradled against his upper arm as she dozed in the car seat, and said abruptly, 'I gather the boys' father does not live with them?'

With reserve, Iona said, 'No.'

He frowned. 'How often do they see him?'

Iona said stiffly, 'Not often.' Never, actually.

The arrogant features hardened and his mouth thinned. He looked down at the child beside him before saying in a voice that lifted the hair on Iona's neck, 'Does your cousin forbid any communication between them?'

She sent him a cool glance that should have warned him off. 'No.'

Contempt iced his tone, transformed his gaze into golden quartz. 'Whatever the situation between your cousin and the boy's father,' he said austerely, 'they are still his sons, and blameless. To abandon them is the act of a weakling.'

It was also affecting the boys badly, but Iona kept silent about that.

When the car drew to halt outside the apartment building Chloe woke up, crossly demanding that Luke carry her.

Iona soothed her. 'He's paying the taxi driver. We'll be at the apartment soon.'

'I don't want to walk,' Chloe said petulantly. She waited until her father joined them to say, 'Lukas, my legs are tired.'

'If they are too tired to stand while we use the elevator, they are tired enough to go straight to bed.' He smiled down at her. 'And some sleep might sweeten that temper of yours, hmm?'

Relief at his support brought a fleeting smile to Iona's face. After a pouting moment Chloe gave in with good grace, trotting alongside her father, her little hand nestled in the strength of his strong own.

When Iona came out from settling her down for her nap, Luke was out on the terrace, surveying the harbour and the islands beyond. Something in his stance stopped her just inside the huge glass doors. Big and hugely competent, a formidable, dominant man, uncompromising in his power and authority, surely he had the world at his feet?

Yet, for a quite irrational moment, she thought he looked completely and utterly alone.

But when he turned his head and beckoned her to join him, his expression showed nothing beyond lazy appreciation as she came towards him.

A secret excitement bloomed in her. Calm yourself, she commanded acerbically.

In a neutral voice he said, 'This is a beautiful city. Or perhaps I should say it has a beautiful setting.'

'We have no buildings to match the glories of Greece,' she admitted.

'In a setting like this it matters not.' He paused, and when she didn't speak said, 'I am satisfied that I need have no worries about Chloe's wellbeing when you are in charge.'

Startled and pleased, she said, 'Thank you. It's what I've been trained to do.'

'It's more than just training; you have a deft touch with children. I noticed you managed both Angie's sons and Chloe easily, sorting out any small problems before they had a chance to escalate. And the principal of the nursery school you worked at before you left to join your cousin's enterprise gave you a glowing commendation.'

Iona stared speechlessly at him. The references she'd packed that morning were still in her bedroom, waiting to be handed to him.

He lifted a brow and said a little arrogantly, 'Surely you did not expect me to accept you without a security check?'

Iona fought back a bewildering complex of responses. Of course in the world of the mega-rich everyone— especially employees—would be checked and double-checked.

Yet his action had revealed only too clearly her position in his life. Their passionate affair and last night's kiss meant nothing. They'd been lovers—surely he'd learned something about her character then?

Uncompromisingly, Luke continued, 'I trust very few people. Chloe is defenceless, and will be alone with you for long periods of time. I would be failing in my duty if I didn't make sure she'd be safe.'

Iona knew she shouldn't be hurt. Already she was forming bonds with the child, and Luke's love for his daughter was subtly altering her feelings for him. Oh, the physical attraction was as strong as ever—stronger, she thought guiltily—but it was now buttressed by emotions she didn't dare face.

CHAPTER FIVE

IONA looked up and met Luke's hard frown. He said, 'You must have had employers check your references before, especially as you taught at nursery school?'

'Well—yes,' she admitted, because of course he was right. Her objection was purely—and ridiculously—personal. She tried to lighten things with a wry smile and the comment, 'Except for Angie, of course.'

'Sometimes the ones closest to you are the ones who most need watching.' His voice was level and un-inflected, but a note in it sent a cold shiver down her spine.

She said, 'It's all right. I do understand. I was just—taken aback, I suppose.'

'You must have lived a very sheltered life. I want the same for Chloe.'

'Any father would want that for his children,' she said, relieved to get off the topic.

'I am not her father.' He spoke without emphasis, his eyes burnished an opaque gold, unreadable yet somehow ruthless when they met and held hers.

Stunned, Iona stared at him. Before she could order her thoughts words tumbled out. 'Then who…?' She shook her head. 'I don't believe you—the resemblance is so strong.'

Surely not *another* man who refused to acknowledge his child?

As though he could read that horrified thought, he twisted his mouth into a sardonic smile. 'Perhaps you should have run a check on *me*. Chloe is my half-sister.'

'Half-sister?' she said blankly.

He lifted broad shoulders in another rapid Mediterranean shrug. 'I have adopted her. The circumstances don't matter. What is important is that she be kept safe.'

She shook her head, trying to clear it. 'From whom?'

'From anyone who'd try to use her,' he said, his deep voice holding more than a touch of impatience.

'I'm afraid that's not enough information,' she told him quickly. At his frown she went on, 'Surely you understand that if she's in any danger I need to know what form it's likely to take?'

He paused a moment before saying, 'At this moment I do not expect any danger to her, but there is always the possibility her birth father might try to claim her.'

Shocked, she asked involuntarily, 'And her birth father is…?'

'The same man who sired me,' he said coldly, as though she should have known.

Angie's words drifted back into Iona's mind. Something about him leaving his family, to which Iona had replied sarcastically that they'd probably always been there for him in the background.

It seemed she'd been wrong; clearly there'd been a rift of massive proportions. As soon as she got access to a computer she was going to find out more about Luke—*Lukas*—Michelakis.

Until then the situation was beyond her comprehension, so she fixed on one thing. 'It's highly unlikely anyone would try to kidnap her here.'

His expression revealed what he thought of that. 'There is no crime in New Zealand, then?' he asked satirically. 'No families torn apart by feuds?'

'Some feud if an innocent child is endangered by it!'

He paused before saying shortly, 'Her *life* is not in danger.'

One glance at his stern face told her that was all he was prepared to let her know. She said, 'New Zealand's situation makes it difficult to smuggle people. We're a long way from anywhere else, with no land borders, so any kidnapper would have to leave by plane, and security is really tight now.'

Again that shrug, more pronounced this time. 'For some people the world is a small place.'

For the very rich, he meant. What on earth had she become caught up in? Starkly she said, 'The check you ran on me must have indicated I have no experience as a bodyguard.'

'It's not necessary—for the time you are caring for Chloe you will be protected wherever you are.'

'You won't be with us all the time.'

'I'm flattered that you think I'd be protection enough,' he said smoothly, 'but I employ security people for that.'

'Everywhere? At the zoo?'

'Of course,' he said, as though she was being naïve.

Somehow the knowledge tarnished a pleasant memory. She shivered.

He covered the distance between them in one stride and touched her bare arm.

'You are cold,' he said quietly, something in his voice alerting her.

Don't look up!

But a force stronger than her will dragged Iona's gaze to his face. Her breath stilled in her throat. Eyes dilating, she stared up at classical features saved from mere beauty by the hard stamp of intelligence and command. A sensuous awareness quivered between them, transforming his aloof tawny-gold survey into a heated, intent examination.

The light touch of his fingers ran like a caress through her, sending a feverish excitement smoking along every nerve. For a taut second she had to grit her teeth, fighting the need that urged her to sway into his arms, surrender to the potent, mind-numbing charm that would banish all her fears.

But that was no longer enough. She felt as though she were on the edge of a life-altering discovery, a step into the unknown so big and important she instinctively flinched back.

Instantly his smouldering gaze turned icy and his hand dropped away.

Random thoughts whirled dizzily around Iona's brain, and although she retained enough presence of mind to speak, her voice emerged in a husky whisper. 'I'm not cold.'

Desire rode Lukas hard, mingling with something darker and even more reckless. He was far too conscious of the texture of Iona's skin, soft and sleek, and the faint scent that owed nothing to any carefully crafted perfume. She smelt of woman, sweet and seductive; it was one of the things about her that had fascinated him.

He'd never forgotten her passion, her laughter, her quick mind and intriguing, mysterious silences. Warm and companionable, touchingly unawakened for a woman who'd spent six months living with the man she'd intended to marry, she'd kept essential parts of herself hidden behind that maddening reserve.

'Then why are you shivering?' he asked softly.

She lifted huge eyes, mysteriously shadowed a dark, deep blue-green. Eyes to lose your soul in, he thought, feeling the reins of his self-control loosening.

Iona's breath blocked her throat, set her heart drumming in a feverish tattoo.

Yes, please... Oh, please...

As though he'd heard the urgent, mute plea Luke bent his head, his mouth taking hers without mercy in a kiss that transcended the past eighteen months as though they'd never existed.

Last night he had kissed her with a purely physical hunger. This was different; it was like coming home, like following her heart into paradise, like entering a fantasy world where all things were miraculously made right. Dimly, through the surging sensations that fired every cell in her body, Iona recognised that this kiss marked a fundamental change in their relationship.

She had no idea where it was leading—and she didn't care. Ravished by Luke's expertise, she surrendered to the sweet need that clamoured through her.

Until Luke lifted his head and dropped the arms that held her against his hard body, and stepped back to say harshly, 'I am sorry—I should not have done this.'

Assailed by a dislocating awareness of where she was, Iona stared at him, her soul-deep joy fading rapidly as he re-imposed control. That formidable will chilled her right to her vulnerable core.

She stepped back and said in a thin voice, 'You're right—it wasn't sensible.'

'It won't happen again.'

Desperately clutching at the ragged shreds of her self-possession, she drew in a jagged breath. 'Is that a promise?'

Luke's dark brows drew together in a frown. 'You have my word on it,' he said shortly.

His unexpected lack of control angered him; he didn't go in for wild lusts or raging desire. For twelve years he'd disciplined his emotions, reaching into his soul to develop a granite self-sufficiency, relying only on his own strength of character. He'd deliberately chosen his lovers for their sophistication and experience and their inability to be hurt.

And then he'd met Iona, a fair trespasser. Met her, and desired her with a swiftly fierce, unexpected passion. At first he'd thought she fitted his specifications—that she was another compliant, worldly woman who wouldn't expect more than he could give—sex, luxury, and the temporary satisfaction of desire. He'd pursued her and taken her, and it had been—magical.

So magical he'd broken the rules he lived by and asked her to move in with him. Permanence was the last thing he'd thought he'd wanted, yet when she'd run away he'd felt something of the bleak sense of betrayal he'd endured when his father had believed his second wife's lies and disinherited him, cutting him off from everyone he loved and trusted.

Iona was a distraction he couldn't afford right now. He needed to concentrate on this latest effort by his father to wreck his life—one that had a fair chance of succeeding.

But that very attack meant he couldn't—yet—get rid

of Iona. He examined her face. Although his kiss had softened the outline of her lips, her wary, self-contained expression belied their temptation.

Iona looked up, meeting his eyes with heightened colour. 'Your security men must be very inconspicuous. I didn't notice anyone.'

'That's the whole point.'

'I don't think I could ever get accustomed to being watched all the time.'

How easily she could dismiss those moments in his arms! Cynically he told himself it was for the best.

'*You* won't be watched,' he said, wrenching his mind from its absorbed focus on that soft mouth and the lingering sensual impact of her slender litheness against him. 'My security men are paid very well to watch the people around Chloe.'

Stop thinking with your sex, he told himself. If he sent Iona away he'd have to find another temporary nanny to take her place. It would take time he no longer had to find someone like Neelie—middle-aged, sensible, and devoted to her charge. More importantly, someone Chloe liked as well as she clearly liked Iona.

So this leftover emotion had to be mastered. And as he'd never yet felt a passion he couldn't control, he shouldn't fail now.

Coldly he continued, 'Get used to it. You've already accepted the position—I hope you're not thinking of reneging.'

Her lashes fell, hiding those changeable eyes.

'I have power.' Simple words, spoken dispassionately. Interested, he waited for her reaction.

She stepped back, her gaze wide and clear and turbulent—but not with fear. 'Are you by any chance *threatening* me again?' she demanded incredulously.

'I did not threaten you before, and I am not doing so now.'

Iona's stomach performed a complicated manoeuvre. His nearness reached something deep inside her, scrambling her thoughts and churning her emotions. But there was a lot more to Luke Michelakis than a stunning face and a body as honed and strong as an Olympic athlete's.

This man, she thought warily, was dangerous. Dangerous in a way she couldn't put a name to, but that some instinct in her recognised.

'It sounded too close to a threat to ignore,' she said stubbornly.

He turned away and looked out across the harbour, unwittingly giving her an excellent view of a profile that could have been taken from an ancient statue.

Indignation at his dismissive action made her lose caution. 'How *dare* you?'

Luke held up a lean, tanned hand. 'Spare me the histrionics,' he said in a bored tone. 'If you're so prone to jumping to conclusions you're not the right person for Chloe.'

Iona stopped her first impetuous response. Angie needed the money, but that wasn't everything. Luke had influence. A word from him might put more work Angie's way.

Or remove it...

Slowly she said, 'And that remark skates very close to blackmail.'

'Are you always this blunt?' He sounded amused.

Chagrined, she darted a glance his way. Darn it, he was laughing at her! And she was being foolish. If she'd thought about it she'd have realised that he'd have security people; she hadn't thought about it because she'd been too overwhelmed by meeting Luke again.

She said, 'I like to know exactly where I am.'

'So do I. I am not threatening you or blackmailing you, so make up your mind. Now.'

She took a deep breath, feeling oddly unsafe, as though she were venturing into thick fog. 'I'm not planning to walk away from our agreement. I'll take care of Chloe while you're in New Zealand, bodyguards or no bodyguards.'

'Good.' Clearly tired of the discussion, he changed the subject. 'I understand this cold spell will go on for several days yet, so after I've finished what I intend to do here we'll go down to the Volcanic Plateau. I'm told the skiing is excellent there still, and Chloe wants to play in the snow. Do you have suitable gear?'

'No, but—'

'Buy some,' Luke said, adding, 'I will of course pay.'

'You don't need to,' she said shortly. 'I'll borrow from my cousin.'

He lifted an eyebrow and inspected her—a look that sent little sizzles of highly suspect anticipation through her.

Luke asked, 'Will they fit? Your cousin has a more voluptuous figure than yours.'

'She calls it matronly,' Iona said staidly. 'I can wear her clothes.' She certainly wasn't going to buy gear Luke would paid for, stuff she might never wear again.

He gave a short nod. 'Check Chloe's wardrobe, please. Neelie knew a trip to the mountains was possible, so there should be suitable garb for Chloe, but make sure. We'll be coming back here, so she won't need to take everything.'

* * *

That night, after she'd put Chloe to bed, Iona closed the door quietly behind her. She was going to miss the little girl when it came time to say goodbye.

Walking outside onto the terrace, she looked around. No sign of Luke, who'd retired to his room. Stomach tightening, she rang Angie.

'Of course you can borrow my skiing clothes, although you'll look a bit of a trick in them—I'm a size bigger than you are,' Angie confirmed.

'That doesn't matter,' Iona said before asking her bluntly, 'Angie, would it be easier for you if I found another job?'

The slight pause before her cousin responded gave her the answer. 'Why are you asking?' Angie asked cautiously. 'Has Lukas offered you a permanent job?'

'No.' She didn't say she wouldn't take the job even if Luke did offer it. His kisses had warned her it would be altogether too risky. 'I don't want to be a drag on you.'

Angie's protest was immediate. 'You could never be that.'

'I can hear the *but*,' Iona told her. 'Tell me now.'

Another pause, as meaningful as the first one. 'Well, last night Felton rang me to say he's not paying support for the boys any more. He's in Australia, so I have no way of forcing him to cough up.'

'The rat,' Iona said with venom. 'Look, as soon as this interlude with Chloe and Luke is over I'll start applying for situations. I won't have any problems getting kindergarten relief work. And while I'm doing that I could relieve at crèches and daycare centres too.'

'You'll take a big drop in income,' Angie said bluntly, but she didn't protest.

'I'll manage.'

Her cousin said, 'I won't deny that it would be—easier. But I feel a heel.'

'Rubbish!'

Her cousin's voice altered, became brisk. 'Don't worry about us—just have fun living the life of the rich while you can. I'll bet this recession hasn't affected Luke Michelakis's net worth by a cent.'

Frowning, Iona set her telephone down, jumping when Luke said from behind her, 'Who is the rat?'

'How do you do that?' she demanded, whirling around to stare at him. He'd discarded his jacket and tie, and the trousers of his business suit hugged his hips and long, heavily muscled thighs like a lover.

His brows shot up. 'Do what?'

'Sneak up on people without a sound.'

'It's not deliberate; it's just my natural gait. Who is this rat you hate so much?'

Unwilling to tell him more about Angie's situation, Iona said glibly, 'An unfaithful husband, that's all.'

It was the truth, but she felt uncomfortable under his steady glaze, and was almost glad when Chloe began to cry in her bedroom.

She'd been sick, and during that night and the next day she endured a virus that kept her in bed and stretched Iona's skills at keeping a fretful child entertained and happy. However, with the miraculous recuperative powers of children, Chloe bounced back late in the afternoon. She was sitting on the terrace under Iona's eye, intent on a picture of the lion she'd seen at the zoo, when Luke strolled out into the sun. He'd taken off his jacket and tie and rolled up his sleeves, and he looked blatantly, sensually male, the hard angles of his face softening when he saw his daughter.

Something very strange melted Iona's spine and

swirled in the pit of her stomach. And her foolish brain seized up under an urgent onrush of need, sharp and penetrating, that filled her with precarious pleasure.

The decision to stay on as Chloe's nanny had been a reckless mistake; each day that passed put her heart in more danger.

'So, you are up,' he said to Chloe, catching her in his arms when she came running towards him, little face radiant.

'I'm better,' she told him earnestly after she'd kissed him. 'I'm not sick now. When can we go to the snow?'

He set her down. 'When the doctor says you are well enough.'

She nodded and dragged him across to see her drawing. Telling her unruly pulse to calm down, Iona stood up.

After a swift glance her way, Luke asked, 'How has she been?'

'For the last two hours, as you see. No sign of a temperature, no aches, no pains, and an appetite that would do credit to a shearer.' When his brows climbed, she enlarged, 'They shear sheep, starting at dawn, and they eat six meals a day. *Large* meals.'

'We have sheep in Greece,' he said mildly. 'The doctor can check her over tomorrow morning to see if she's fit to travel.'

'I want to go to the snow,' Chloe said eagerly.

He frowned. 'Little one, you will go wherever the good doctor says is best for you.' Chloe looked pleadingly up at him, but he turned his attention back to Iona. 'I will be out tonight. However, tomorrow I'll be at home in good time, so you can take the afternoon and the evening off. You have been in constant attendance on this small tyrant here, and no doubt you have things to do.'

'Thank you,' she said automatically.

She did have things to do, and she also wanted to talk to her cousin. Angie's ex-husband's refusal to pay maintenance was upsetting but not unexpected; it had reinforced Iona's decision to find another job—a decision she spent the next evening discussing with Angie, who reluctantly accepted it.

Feeling wrung out, Iona said, 'Angie, before I go can I use your computer?'

'Of course.'

An hour later Iona closed the computer and looked up as Angie came into the small bedroom she'd converted into an office. 'You look a bit green around the gills,' her cousin said, frowning. 'What have you been doing?'

'Researching Luke.'

Angie's concern deepened into active worry. 'What have you found? Something nasty?'

'Yes. Oh, not Luke.' Angie gave her a concerned look. Hastily she explained, 'The reason for his family bust-up.' She hesitated, then said reluctantly, 'His father is Aristo Michelakis, the shipping magnate. Apparently he claims descent from Hippolytus.'

Angie looked surprised. 'Who?'

Iona shivered. 'It's a Greek myth. Or perhaps ancient history. Anyway, Hippolytus was the son of the king of Athens. His stepmother fell in love with him, but when he spurned her she claimed he raped her, and then hung herself. The king killed his son.'

'Charming,' Angie said with emphasis. 'I hope fervently this has nothing to do with Luke's departure from the family home.'

'Unfortunately it has.' Iona swallowed. 'Luke's mother died when he was seventeen, and Aristo almost immediately married his much-younger secretary—a blonde with a very hard face, judging by the photos. A year or so later she apparently told her husband that Luke had either seduced or raped her—the reports skirt around that aspect, but it was easy enough to read between the lines. The stepmother took an overdose. She didn't die, but Aristo divorced her immediately.'

'Ugh. And uncanny.'

'Horrible.' Iona still felt sick. She switched off the computer and stood up.

Angie said, 'At least Luke's father didn't kill him.'

'No, he just booted Luke out of the family—cast him adrift with no money except a legacy from his maternal grandfather.'

'Very nasty indeed,' Angie agreed.

Iona got to her feet and said abruptly, 'I rather wish I hadn't decided to pry. How could Luke's father *do* that?'

Angie looked at her with an equivocal expression. 'Perhaps it was the *old bull being tossed out of the herd by the younger one* syndrome.'

'Syndrome or not, nothing can excuse him. No wonder Luke's so—so tough,' Iona said forthrightly.

'You sound quite convinced that he didn't do whatever he was supposed to have done.'

Iona stared at her cousin, her expression stunned. 'Of course I am,' she said numbly. But why?

Angie asked curiously, 'I thought—you let me think—you didn't know him very well. What makes you so sure he's incapable of committing adultery with his stepmother? Or raping her, come to that.'

'I know he wouldn't,' Iona said, shocked by her

cousin's bluntness. 'I know it sounds silly, but he's just not the sort.' She glanced at her watch. 'I have to go now. We're off tomorrow morning. I'll keep in touch.'

'Be careful, all right?'

'I'm always careful.' But she needed to be much more than careful now.

CHAPTER SIX

LUKE opened the door to her when she arrived back. He'd changed into a short-sleeved shirt striped the same tawny colour as his eyes, and he looked slightly rumpled, an informality increased by the darkish shadow of a beard around his lean jaw. Sensation sizzled deep in the pit of Iona's stomach—desire made even more intense by what she'd just discovered.

How could his father have thrown him out? It beggared belief.

Although Aristo Michelakis did seem to make a habit of rejecting his children. Now she understood why Luke had adopted his baby half-sister, and she honoured him for it.

What was wrong with his father? Couldn't he see what he'd done to his children?

Luke stepped aside to let her in, then examined her so intently she shifted uncomfortably. Her research now seemed an intolerable intrusion into his life.

He asked, 'Have you had a good evening?'

'Yes, thank you.' And was that ever a lie!

'Good.' He waited until they had almost reached the door of her room before saying, 'I am about to make myself a drink. Would you like to join me?'

Just beyond her door stood another table, not as

opulent as the one in the foyer. During the day some-one had come in to change the flowers, replacing them with a great bowl of roses. A large mirror reflected their elegant blooms and their scent charged the air with a seductively heavy perfume. Several petals had fallen from one, the matt golden forms trailing so artistically across the polished wood it looked as though it had been deliberately done.

Temptation warred with caution. Caution won, but only by a whisker. Iona said, 'Actually, I'm tired. I'll go straight to my room, thank you.'

'Perhaps that is wise,' Luke said negligently, clearly not in the least put out.

She turned to go, then asked, 'What time do we leave in the morning?'

'About nine.' He stooped to pick up several petals from the floor.

Iona tore her eyes away from the slow flex and coil of powerful muscles beneath the linen of his shirt. Her heart was pumping blood feverishly through her, so loudly she could hear it beating in her ears.

Luke said, 'Do you ski?'

'Yes.'

'Then you will enjoy the next few days. We'll hire boots for you when we get there.'

She said, 'Surely I'll be looking after Chloe?'

A subtle current of communication vibrated between them—a kind of subliminal exchange both desperately exciting and immediate. He kept his distance, but she felt the impact of his gaze in every cell.

'I thought the doctor told you she was perfectly all right to holiday on the mountain?' he said.

'Yes. Yes, he did.'

He didn't even have to touch her, she thought in

confusion, to set her alight. She was so aware of him she felt adrenalin surge through her veins, a drugging anticipation preparing her for him.

'Then, although you will spend quite a bit of time with her, there will be occasions when you can ski if you want to.'

Sex with Luke had taught her that until she'd met him she'd only dabbled in love. With Gavin it had begun as friendship, deepening slowly and inevitably, sweetly and surely, into something deeper. Her only lover before Luke, he'd been gentle and patient, tenderly initiating her.

Luke had demanded a sensual energy to match his own. And she'd found it, surrendering to a sexuality that summoned something wild and unrestrained from her, a passionate yielding to the moment. He'd encouraged her to follow her impulses, to take control sometimes, to explore his body and her own with elemental, tantalising appetite until she lost all sense of self.

His generosity was part of the reason she didn't believe he'd wrecked his family. And her sweetly desperate expectation was one impulse she was not going to follow. If she did, she risked so much more—her heart and her happiness.

After dragging a sharp breath into starving lungs, she said, 'I'll go and pack now.'

She went past him, only to be stopped by a lazy hand that just grazed her forearm. Rills of sensation tightened her skin.

He dropped his hand and said lazily, 'The drink I intended to have is to celebrate a very good deal I signed today with your Prime Minister and his attendant army of civil servants and advisors. Good for me, good for

New Zealand. I don't drink alone, so I'd like you to share it with me.'

'Is that an order?' she asked, because temptation had come roaring back.

He shrugged and said indifferently, 'Of course not.'

Say no. Say no right now…

But what harm could there be in sharing a drink with him? It seemed mean to deny him the pleasure of celebrating. 'In that case, and because this deal is going to be good for New Zealand, I'll join you,' she said sedately.

In the sitting room he poured champagne, and handed a flute of the scintillating wine to her, saying with a gleam of amusement in his lion eyes, 'If you were always as blunt as you are now, you must have been an interesting child.'

Iona smiled ruefully. 'Tact and discretion did come hard. I probably embarrassed my parents until I learned the boundaries.'

'Childhood is a time for exploring life, and one for learning boundaries too.' He gave a sudden wry smile. 'And a parent both explores and learns too. It came as a considerable shock to me to find that children have a definite personality right from birth.'

Of course, he'd been an only child. 'She's a credit to you.'

'She is a credit to herself,' he corrected. 'I made every mistake possible in her first year, when I cared for her myself, yet she managed to thrive in spite of my ineptitude.'

Startled, Iona looked up. 'You looked after her yourself?' At his nod she asked, 'Why?'

He gave that slight, very Mediterranean shrug. 'I read

several books, and found that it is important for a child to bond with someone in their first year. I wanted it to be me, not a nanny who might leave in the future, so I took her to the island—my real home. Thanks to modern communications conducting business was simple enough from there.' He gave a reminiscent smile. 'Looking after a baby was not so easy, but between us—and with the help of several very experienced island grandmothers and mothers—Chloe and I managed.'

Stunned and oddly touched, Iona said, 'Well, between you all you've done a brilliant job.'

He saluted her with his glass. 'Here's to Chloe, then. And also to... Well, I shan't pre-empt the Prime Minister's announcement tomorrow, so let's call it a toast to a chance to make a difference.'

Startled, she echoed his toast and sipped wine that set her tastebuds tingling with delight. Only the very best for Luke Michelakis, she thought, trying to rein in her runaway reaction to his presence. Everything seemed stronger, more vivid, more potent—from the wine to the man who looked down at her with half-closed eyes.

He set his glass down and said, 'So...boundaries. Perhaps we should establish some too.'

No touching, she thought hurriedly, then flushed, because of course he wasn't thinking of that sort of boundary. She was his employee.

Luke went on, 'While you are in my care you will be treated like one of the family.'

'In your *care*?' she asked, stunned. She gave a wry laugh. 'That's a very old-fashioned, rather patriarchal way of looking at the situation. You're my employer.'

'I was brought up in a patriarchal society,' he told her coolly. 'It is entirely natural for me to think like that.'

'Do you consider it your duty to care for every one of your employees?'

'In a less personal fashion,' he admitted with a wry smile. 'You live in my house and care for Chloe, so it is different, but, yes, I ensure that not only do the people I employ have good working conditions, but that they are taken care of in other ways. I support an excellent pension plan and health scheme.'

She said briskly, 'Well, as this is a temporary job you won't have to enrol me. New Zealand has a good healthcare system, and of course we have universal superannuation.'

Luke thought ironically that he'd never have believed he'd drink champagne with a woman—one he wanted with a taut, driving intensity that kept him awake at nights—and talk about such dull subjects as pension plans and health schemes.

Not that he should be surprised. Iona had never fitted into any of his categories; as a lover she'd been passionate and sensuous, but she'd left him without a backwards glance.

And now, he thought, making a swift decision, was the right time to ask the reason.

'Why did you run away from Tahiti?' His tone was idly enquiring.

She gave him a shadowed glance, hesitated, then said slowly, 'I wasn't ready for anything else.'

And now? It suddenly became important to him to probe further, but he sensed that now was the wrong time. 'Because of the death of your fiancé?'

She said quietly, 'Yes, but also—my parents had died in a car accident that year. And Angie's marriage broke up around the same time. Everything I valued—everyone I loved—was either dead or in great distress.'

Her narrow brows drew together. Not quite looking at him, she said, 'I didn't dare stay. I was afraid.'

'I see.' He understood how great loss could have made her unable to trust her instincts, and stifled the urge to comfort her. She wasn't ready for that, either.

Lashes lowered, she was sipping the champagne with delicate pleasure. His whole body tightened, so that he had to lock every muscle to stop himself from going over and taking the glass from her hand, pulling her into his arms, kissing that softly lush mouth until it parted for him...

What would she do?

Respond, he thought with brutal honesty. She'd go up in flames—yet, although he could take her physically, she'd keep him shut out from her emotions and her thoughts. For reasons he wasn't prepared to explore he had an uncivilised, reckless need to shatter those barriers, compel her to see him not as a man she was unwillingly attracted to, but as a lover who meant something to her.

Was she going to hold the memory of her fiancé in her heart for the rest of her life? How could any man compete with a dead hero?

His mind went back to the conversation he'd just had with Neelie. Now was not the time to reveal the nanny's decision, he decided.

The next few days on the mountain would give him time to test his ability to resist Iona. If she proved too tempting, he'd—well, he'd face that if he was forced to.

Aloud he said, 'I hadn't realised your parents died so tragically and so soon after your fiancé's death. I'm sorry.'

She blinked, then said with difficulty, 'You gave

me something in Tahiti.' Colour burned along her cheekbones and she hurried on, 'And not just the— our relationship. I found that I could feel again, that I could enjoy things and respond to them. Thank you for that.'

It was a start.

Iona surveyed the view from the sitting room window. Clouds of pale mist rising from the base of the tall trees that surrounded the lodge gave the garden a mysterious, almost eerie air.

The man who'd showed them to their rooms said, 'That's steam from the hot springs. There are several pools, all entirely natural, and tested every day to make sure they stay pure. Soaking in the water is a wonderful way to ease out the stiffness after a day on the mountain. And there's one that's very suitable for children.'

Chloe looked hopefully up at her father, who said, 'Later, perhaps.'

Iona looked around the luxurious room. Although as casually sophisticated, the house in Tahiti had possessed a totally different ambience, tropical and beachy. Here a creative decorator had furnished the rooms with native timbers, their rich warmth set off by serene hues taken from sky and bush. Skilfully placed accents in the earthy colours of the volcanic area provided a vital contrast, as did some seriously good art.

Of course it was luxurious—a splendidly equipped lodge set up for several groups of visitors, although they were the only occupants. Their upstairs suite had its own entrance and foyer, with several bedrooms. Iona's was beside Chloe's, with one for Luke on the other side.

The bodyguard, a serious young man with a faint American accent, had been introduced as Iakobos. 'Just

Iakobos?' Iona had asked with a smile as she'd extended her hand.

After a glance at Luke he'd shaken it somewhat gingerly. 'Just Iakobos, ma'am,' he'd said.

Chloe clearly knew and liked him, and he'd crouched down to say, 'Hi, Chloe. You're growing up, young lady.'

Then he had melted into the background, something he was clearly very good at.

'What standard is your skiing?' Luke asked later, when Chloe was taking her nap.

'I used to be reasonably proficient as a schoolgirl, but I'm well out of practice.' Iona gave him a questioning look, meeting his eyes with a sharp shift of awareness that twanged along her nerves. 'It doesn't matter, surely? I'll be spending my time on the nursery slopes with Chloe.'

'Tomorrow morning, yes, that is correct. So she gets to know the instructor,' Luke said shortly. 'After that there will be times when you can ski at your level while Iakobos stays with her.'

Luke spent the rest of the afternoon in a room that functioned as an office; at one stage Iona heard him speaking in what she presumed to be Greek. A momentary gleam of compassion at his having to work on what was clearly meant to be a holiday was stifled when his tone changed, dropping into a silky quietness that sent a cold shiver down her spine.

Very glad she wasn't the person he was talking to, she took Chloe to explore the grounds of the lodge, Iakobos a silent presence with them.

Of course they made snowballs, Chloe showing a streak of mischief by tossing them at both Iona and the bodyguard. Iona could see why the child liked the young man; he entered fully into the spirit of the occasion, teasing her in a mixture of Greek and English and making her laugh.

'You know how to deal with children,' Iona said as he directed a small snowball towards Chloe.

It hit her in the stomach, exploding over in her in a flurry, and she sat down abruptly in the snow. After a moment of shock her face crinkled into laughter.

'I am the oldest in our family,' he said, hiding a smile as he watched Chloe snatch up handfuls of snow, obviously bent on retaliation. 'And she is a charming child, easy to deal with and to like.'

Indeed she was; they both pretended not to see her busily moulding a snowball, her face intent and serious.

'I think you're going to be attacked,' Iona observed.

He smiled down at her. He had a very nice smile, and he was a good-looking man, yet for some reason he didn't affect her at all. Not like Luke...

'Miss Guthrie—?'

'Call me Iona,' she said swiftly.

He didn't appear to have heard. 'When she throws, she will aim at me, which means it will almost certainly hit you,' he warned.

Iona's laughter was cut short by a level voice from behind.

Luke. In the same silkily lethal tone she'd heard before he said, 'I assume you think it's perfectly all right for Chloe to be sitting on the cold ground?'

Both Iona and the bodyguard whirled, Iona resisting an unnecessary guilt.

How could a golden gaze splinter into ice? Luke's face was like a mask, the angular features set in forbidding lines until Chloe abandoned her snowball and scrambled to her feet, hurling herself at him with a yelp of glee.

His expression softening, he picked her up and in a totally different voice he said, 'Are you cold?'

'Only my nose is,' she said cheerfully, and touched his. 'So's yours,' she said, and started to laugh before breaking into another language.

'English,' he said sternly. 'Miss Iona doesn't understand Greek.'

Obediently she switched, her words tumbling out. 'We've been playing snowballs. Iakobos threw one and it hit me in the tummy, so I was going to hit him with a big, big one.' She held out her arms to indicate just how huge it had been going to be.

'Perhaps you can try that tomorrow. For now, it's time for us to take our cold noses inside,' Luke said, and strode back towards the house with her in his arms.

Still feeling chastened, Iona fell in behind, Iakobos beside her. Within seconds Luke called the bodyguard to walk beside him.

Glowering at their backs, Iona told herself she'd done nothing that could be construed as a lack of care or duty. So why was Luke so angry? Was he still furious with the unlucky person on the other end of the telephone? Surely he wasn't one of those people who let their emotions splatter onto everyone around them?

She was obscurely disappointed. It showed a lack of self-control, something she hadn't expected of him.

And why should she care? Because she was getting too involved with him, that was why. She stumbled, righting herself rapidly as Luke turned.

'Take care,' he commanded. 'The path is slippery.'

It was, but that wasn't why she'd tripped. The sensual attraction that throbbed between them was being transformed into something new and powerful. Oh, the elemental sexual pull was still as strong as ever—no, stronger—but it was now grounded in deeper and more significant emotions. Watching him with Chloe and seeing him with Angie's boys, reading how his father had rejected him—even the conversation about taking care of his workers—had altered her perceptions.

In Tahiti it had all been about lust.

Now she wanted more. She was halfway to falling in love with Lukas Michelakis, internet tycoon, father, disgraced son, respected businessman...

She lifted her eyes, letting them linger on his broad shoulders and narrow hips, measuring the relaxed, ground-covering gait that spoke of strength and power, noting the way he held his child, the swift smile he gave her, his tenderness.

Halfway?

Panic kicked beneath her ribs and hollowed out her stomach as she reacted to a shocking flash of comprehension. Somehow, at some unknown time, ignoring any warning signs, she'd fallen the whole way in love with Luke. She wanted love and marriage and a life together.

And Lukas Michelakis was about as far out of her reach as—well, as the stars.

To him she was that most ex of all exes: an ex-lover. Oh, he still desired her, but it wasn't in the same all-consuming way she wanted him. He could control that. And soon she'd be an ex-employee, someone temporary and peripheral, only remembered because she'd been useful to him.

The emptiness in her heart expanded, cold with foreboding. She'd have to pick up the pieces of her life again—although this time, she thought as she bustled

Chloe off for a bath and to change her clothes, there would be no guilt.

That thought didn't console her, but getting the child ready for dinner and bed at least gave her something else to concentrate on.

After the nursery tea Luke came in to kiss Chloe goodnight. Apart from a short nod he ignored Iona, until they were back in the sitting room of the suite.

'I'm eating out,' he said. 'Your dinner will be brought to you here.'

'Very well, sir,' she returned, her voice expressionless.

He stopped in mid-stride. 'What did you call me?' he demanded.

Already regretting the foolish impulse, she said, 'I noticed Iakobos calls you that, so I thought perhaps it was mandatory.'

His eyes narrowed. 'You appear to have noticed a lot about him,' he said conversationally. He walked across to the door and opened it. 'I don't want to hear that again. Just remember you are here to care for Chloe, not to flirt with the bodyguard.'

'Flirt?' she sputtered, welcoming the swift rush of temper. '*Flirt?* Poor Chloe—if you think that was flirting, you're going to have a difficult time of it when she becomes interested in the opposite sex. And so is she.'

He said curtly, 'Leave Chloe out of it. You forget I have seen the way you approach a man—I have noticed the promise in your smile, the sway of your hips, the upward glance from beneath your lashes.'

His coolly dismissive words stung, yet Iona recognised a raw undernote to them. Her breath locked in her throat when she caught the hard flame of hunger in his scrutiny. Her pulses thundered and a hot surge of physical longing plunged her into confusion.

He'd never love her, but he still wanted her.

Luke smiled cynically. 'It is difficult to hide from passion—our bodies betray us all the time.' He let his gaze drift from her wide, darkening eyes to the curves of her breast and waist.

Shocked by the violence of her headstrong response— so close to craving she didn't dare say anything in case she revealed the hot tide his words had unleashed within her—Iona stared mutely at him, pulses leaping in a mixture of fear and eagerness.

No.

Any surrender now would be infinitely rash—far more reckless than those moon-dazed nights in Tahiti. The only way she could keep her self-respect was to ignore the compelling lure of passion—especially now that it was reinforced by a love that had crept upon her so slowly she hadn't realised its danger until far too late.

Yet it took every ounce of will power she possessed for her to drag in a sighing breath and shake her head.

'You disagree with me?' he asked softly, and touched the betraying little throb at the base of her throat.

Fire beat up through her, and she couldn't tear her eyes away from his, drowning in hot gold. He was judging her reactions with an expert's experience.

That thought pulled her up instantly. Swallowing hard, she managed to step back, vainly trying to armour herself against his powerful male potency. A violent yearning fogged her mind and reminded her how good— how *very* good—it had been to forget everything in the safe haven of his arms.

Her voice slow and uncertain, she said, 'I don't pretend to have your vast knowledge of sex and sexuality.' The words sounded too much like a come-on, and she stopped, took another breath and started again. 'But what's past is gone. It's over and done with.'

'Surely we've both accepted that it's not?' The hint of amusement in his words set her teeth on edge, intensifying when he added, 'This need is very much present. You can't deny that.'

Iona shook her head, trying to clear her mind from the drugging fumes of desire. 'It's a waste of time—and foolish—to let the past impinge on the present.'

'How can you stop it?' His tone was suddenly abrupt. 'The past is always there. It never leaves us. Everything we do, everything we say, every thought and emotion and sensation is directly affected by what has happened to us previously.' He looked down at her. 'You don't believe me? Then think about this—'

He bent and his lips brushed hers for a second, sending sharp darts of fire through her. Iona tensed, but he lifted his head immediately and stepped back, leaving her tingling, her lips tender and aching for more.

Luke smiled with cold irony. 'If you had never lain in my arms, never kissed me with all of that passion you're trying to conceal, you wouldn't be so defensive now, and your body wouldn't be remembering what pleasure we found in each other. We can't escape the past, Iona.'

She said harshly, 'Perhaps not, but we don't need to repeat it.'

'I agree.' His expression hardened. As a jolt of keen pain seared through her, he went on, 'You have a pretty name; in Greek it would refer to the violet—either its colour or the flower itself—valued for its modest beauty and retiring disposition.'

Something in his voice and the gleam in his lion-tawny eyes told her he didn't think the name suited her.

Feeling stupid and callow, she turned away, tense until she heard the quiet huff of the closing door. Even then she couldn't relax. The cold certainty in his voice when he'd spoken of the past made her shiver. Clearly he could never forgive his father.

She walked across to the window and stared out at the wild landscape outside—snow against black rocks, the dark, mysterious shapes of the trees silhouetted against steam formed in the heart of the earth and forced into the cold air.

She closed her eyes. Somehow she had to conquer this—this newfound love. It was embarrassing. Demeaning, even.

And scary.

Each time he'd kissed her she'd blazed up like dry tinder—like a woman who had met her one true love after long years of separation, everything forgotten in the rapturous joy of reunion.

Whereas he'd been master of the situation.

CHAPTER SEVEN

HEAT burned across Iona's cheekbones, replaced by the chill of humiliation. 'Face it,' she said aloud. 'You responded like a wanton, and he recognised it and stepped back before things got out of hand.'

She gripped the edge of the sill, knuckles whitening. Perhaps she should give in, let things take their course. Her breath quickened in time with her heartbeat. But even as temptation filled her mind with dazzling, seductive images, with memories that still had the power to corrode her will, she rejected it.

It might work—if only she hadn't fallen in love with him.

Torn between stunned joy at this unexpected love and a shadowy fear that made a coward of her, she turned away, letting the curtains fall to close out the night.

Cravenly, she made sure she went to bed well before the time Luke was likely to return. She even managed to fall asleep—although she woke when she thought she heard him go past her door, and it took her quite a while afterwards to settle.

Later—much later—she woke in a rush, her heart thudding unpleasantly, unable to place herself. The chilly grey light of dawn was sifting through the curtains, and she stared round the room, fragmented snippets of a dream playing through her thoughts.

Gavin, she thought incredulously, and shivered in the warm room, because since the last night in Tahiti the dreams had stopped. She no longer relived over and over again the moment when he'd used the last of his strength to push her up onto the safety of the rocks, then surrendered to the waves that dragged him relentlessly under.

This time it hadn't been the nightmare; he'd been sailing on a blue sea, a lazy sun washing the beloved lines of his face with soft gold, and he'd been smiling...

No, she thought with a reminiscent little smile of her own, he'd been *grinning*—the way he always had when the wind and the sea and his yacht had been in perfect tune together. He'd looked completely happy.

Wish fulfilment on her part? Or a final relinquishment brought about by her new-found love for Luke?

Restlessly she got out of bed and paced across to the window, pushing back the curtains.

The scene outside drove away the already fading images from her dream; probably the last snowfall before summer had drifted down overnight, covering the mountain in a soft white cloak and almost hiding the jagged rocks formed by old eruptions.

In the distance, high above the lodge, the irregular peak emitted a faint white plume of steam, white against the brightening sky, ethereal and gauzily sinister. Although beautiful and sacred to local Maori, Ruapehu was an active volcano. It had killed before; it would probably do so again.

Shivering, Iona checked the time; she'd better shower and get ready for the day.

They were having breakfast when Luke emerged

from the study. After dropping a kiss on Chloe's cheek, he said, 'Good morning, Iona,' as he straightened, and fixed her with a cool look. 'I trust you don't plan to wear jeans on the mountain?'

'No.' She hoped he couldn't see her inner agitation. 'They have about as much cold and wind resistance as tissue paper.'

He nodded. 'Good. I'm heli-skiing today, but I'll go with you up the chairlift to the beginners' slopes.' A glance at his watch made him frown. 'In half an hour?'

'We'll be ready,' Iona told him. Heli-skiing? Did he know the mountain well enough to go off piste?

Common sense told her it was ridiculous to worry about him. He'd have a guide.

Half an hour later one glance at him reassured her that he knew what he was doing. His clothes were weatherproof, practical, and well-worn. That they emphasised his shoulders and long legs was purely coincidental, and his masculine virility even managed to overcome the effect of heavy boots and a traditional hat.

He was dangerously, heart-shakingly sexy.

Whereas she looked odd in Angie's gear; the colours were wrong and it bunched uneasily on her.

Who cared? Luke gave her one swift glance, as though to reassure himself, before asking, 'Is Chloe ready?'

'Almost.'

Chloe had wanted to wear a bright pink all-in-one snowsuit. She'd pouted when Iona had suggested she'd be too cold out in the wind, but obediently accepted a jacket with a warm hood. She looked enchanting.

Iona's heart contracted. *Careful*, she warned herself

as they took the lift down. *In a few days you'll wave goodbye, and probably never see her again.*

Unless some time in the future she figured in a society wedding of the year, or got caught up in some scandal that made the sort of headlines Iona had read researching Luke and his family.

That didn't seem at all likely, not with a father like Luke!

He stayed with Iona and Chloe for half an hour or so, watching Chloe's progress on the beginners' slopes before kissing her goodbye. He straightened and said austerely, 'I'll see you later,' to Iona.

It felt like a rebuff, but she nodded. He looked at Iakobos, and the two of them walked some distance away and talked for a few minutes before Luke left.

It was idiotic to feel abandoned. Iona forced herself to concentrate on the peaceful, pleasant morning. Chloe showed she had good co-ordination for a three-year-old, and her beaming face shone with delight as she demonstrated her skills. Although Iakobos didn't seem to be around much, Iona had no doubt they were under surveillance.

And, no matter how hard she tried to reason it away, at the back of her mind lurked a glimmer of worry about Luke.

Once the session was over she agreed to Chloe's appeal to eat lunch at the café with Iakobos, then took the now yawning child back to the lodge and settled her for her nap.

She checked her cell phone, sent a text message to Angie telling her everything was fine and thanking her for the loan of her clothes. Then she stood at the window and looked up the mountain, wondering where Luke was.

It was utterly foolish to be flooded with relief when he returned. After greeting her coolly, he closeted himself in the room he used as an office.

Much to Chloe's disappointment, he was still in there when she woke. Once she'd gobbled a piece of fruit and a glass of milk she had to be dissuaded from knocking on the door, and by the time he finally emerged Iona had coaxed her to help put together a jigsaw.

The sound of his door opening had Chloe scrambling to her feet, her face lighting up as she ran to him, chattering in Greek.

'English, Chloe,' he said firmly, then looked across at Iona. 'What is this zoo?'

'It's a petting zoo—it has farm animals for children to stroke and learn about.'

'Can we go, Luke?' Chloe pleaded. 'There's lambs there, and little calves to suck your fingers, and some puppies and baby...' She stopped, screwed up her face, then used a Greek word.

'Rabbits,' Luke supplied. He looked at Iona. 'Where is this place?'

Iona said, 'Quite close, I believe—on the other side of the village.'

He paused a moment, then said abruptly, 'Iakobos will drive you there.'

Chloe pouted, although one look at his severe face kept her silent. However, he explained, 'I have calls to make, little one—important calls.'

In spite of his absence, the petting zoo was a success. Chloe loved the animals, and was smiling blissfully as she stroked a small black rabbit when a woman gushed from behind Iona, 'Your daughter is such a pretty child—a real charmer.'

Iona turned around, but before she could say anything

Iakobos cut in smoothly, 'Thank you. We think she is just about perfect, but of course we are biased.'

The woman was middle-aged and talkative, glancing from Iona to Iakobos. She laughed and said, 'All parents are biased. Are you on holiday?'

'Yes,' Iakobos said, and smiled down at Iona with warmth.

The friendly inquisition continued. 'Oh, you're Americans, are you? How are you enjoying New Zealand?'

'We're thoroughly enjoying your lovely country,' he told her, his American accent a little more pronounced. 'Time to go now, sweetheart.'

The words were addressed to both Iona and Chloe, who set the rabbit down carefully and scrambled to her feet, her face revealing an expression that reminded Iona very much of her half-brother when he was angry.

The woman said, 'Enjoy the rest of your holiday, then,' and beamed at them.

Iona held out her hand, but Chloe ignored it, stamping along beside her while they made their way to the car. Above her head, Iona said, 'What was that about?'

Iakobos had reverted to being a bodyguard. He opened the car door and settled them in, then got in behind the wheel. 'Nothing,' he said calmly, switching on the engine. 'Are all people so curious here?'

She lifted her brows and said with a touch of frost in her tone, 'We're noted for being friendly.'

He said no more on the trip home. And Chloe, gentle, sweet, happy Chloe, was sobbing as she got out of the car. To Iona's surprise the crying increased as they went up to their suite, turning into a tantrum that brought Luke from his office.

Iona had picked up the wildly flailing child, and was

already halfway to her room. Ignoring Luke's grim expression, she said, 'Chloe is over-tired. She'll be much happier once she's had a bath and her dinner.'

Chloe wailed, 'I'm *not* Iakobos's little girl. I belong to Lukas.'

Later, after Chloe had been soothed and reassured enough to follow the familiar routine to bed, Luke asked crisply, 'What the hell was that all about?'

'I didn't realise she'd heard.' Iona related the scene with the over-inquisitive woman. 'Just why did Iakobos feel it was necessary to do that?'

Luke was silent a moment, then said, 'You dealt with her well. It's been some time since Chloe's had a tantrum.'

She said with a wry little smile, 'I've coped with plenty of them. And she'll be growing out of them soon. I can guess why it upset her so, but you didn't answer my question.'

The silence that followed her words was oddly tense. She could feel it tighten her skin, and almost jumped when he spoke. 'I have a proposition to put to you.'

'Another one?'

Her attempt at lightening the atmosphere failed miserably. His shoulders lifted an inch or so, then fell.

'Another one,' he agreed shortly. 'I want you to marry me.'

Shock sent Iona's head spinning. She blinked, tamped down a wild hope, and opened her eyes again. The angular set of Luke's face convinced her that he'd actually said those words. *I want you to marry me...*

But she could read nothing except grim determination in the strong features and flinty eyes.

Something splintered inside her. It might have been

her heart. Still too dizzy to think clearly, she asked baldly, 'Why?'

He turned away and poured a couple of drinks—a glass of the white wine he must have remembered she liked from that holiday in Tahiti, and something considerably stronger for him.

'Here,' he said brusquely, and handed her the glass. 'There are several reasons. Neelie is not going to be able to come back to Chloe in the foreseeable future. Her mother will be an invalid for the rest of her life, and Neelie wishes to care for her.'

Iona took a gulp of her drink, then set the glass down with a sharp clink. 'You don't have to get married for that reason. Good nannies are reasonably easy to find,' she managed to croak. 'For heaven's sake, Angie knows a couple of really top-class ones.'

There had to be more to it than that. Hell, he could simply ask her to take on the job. He didn't have to offer marriage.

Well, *offer* wasn't exactly the right word. It had sounded more like an order than an offer.

With a real effort she reined in her chaotic thoughts.

He too drank from his glass before putting it down. Eyes shielded by his thick lashes, he said, 'I have just received confirmation that my father—who as you know is also Chloe's birth father—is about to sue for custody.'

Appalled, Iona reached for her glass, decided against it and dragged air into her famished lungs. Right now, more than anything, she needed a clear head. 'Why would he do that?'

In a steely, expressionless voice that made his reluctance palpable, Luke told her, 'Until now he has been convinced that I was fooled by his greedy, unfaithful mistress into adopting a child of unknown parentage. He has just found out she is truly his daughter, so he wishes to take her from me.'

And that's enough information, his tone indicated.

No, it wasn't. Outraged, Iona said, 'Just like that—as though she's a discarded plaything? You must be able to arrange a mutually satisfactory solution so that both of you—?'

'No.'

The stark, flat denial cut her composure to shreds. Silenced, she met implacable eyes above a mouth set in an inflexible line.

'He does not want that,' he said. 'And neither do I.'

Iona shook her head, trying to clear it. 'I thought you said he rejected her?'

'He was convinced his mistress had been unfaithful, so he refused to consider the possibility of her child being his.'

And that, his level, emotionless tone told her, was all she'd learn about that. But beneath the words she sensed an anger that sent a shiver scudding the length of her spine.

Nevertheless, she couldn't allow herself to be intimidated into taking such a step—even though some abject part of her was rashly trying to persuade her to accept his proposal.

Marshalling her thoughts, she said, 'Luke, a custody dispute is always better for the child if it is negotiated by both parties. Surely your father and you can come—?'

'This is not simply a custody dispute,' he interrupted, and for a moment she caught a glimpse of deep weariness. It was rapidly replaced by a ruthless lack of compromise.

'So tell me what it is,' she said steadily.

He turned away and stared out of the window. In a voice she'd never heard him use before he said, 'For my father, Chloe is nothing more than a weapon he can use in the ongoing war between us—a war that started when he believed my stepmother's lies and cast me out of the family for ever.'

Whatever his emotions, they were so rigidly controlled she couldn't recognise them. 'I can understand that you're bitter about her lies—'

He turned and fixed her with a stone-hard gaze. 'She accused me of trying to seduce her.'

Iona refused to pretend she didn't know about the old scandal. 'Your father should have known better than to believe her.'

His gaze pierced through her as though he could read the thoughts in her brain, the emotions in her heart. 'My father believes he is a direct descendant of Theseus, king of Athens, who had his son killed for supposedly raping his stepmother. I think he probably believed—still believes—it is a case of history repeating itself.'

'Why?'

He said reluctantly, 'We had been quarrelling—he wanted to control my future, and I was determined to make my own way. He scorned my hopes, my plans, and my ambitions.' He shrugged. 'I was stupidly hotheaded and defiant. And I suspect he was jealous. I was young—he was not. It seems you believe that I didn't do it.'

'Of course I do.' Iona stopped, astounded by the thought of him doubting her. When she'd read the story on Angie's computer screen she'd had no question whatever about Luke's integrity.

Big and dominating and forceful, eyes narrow and

penetrating, Luke said, 'There's no *of course* about it. Why?' His voice was almost indifferent.

'Because I just can't imagine you behaving like that,' she said after several taut seconds had ticked by. It sounded lame, and she added, 'I think it's probably because you're so good with Chloe.'

When his brows lifted sardonically she flushed, trying to explain the inexplicable. 'OK, so it's not much of a reason, but that and sheer gut instinct are the only ones I've got. And the fact that for as long as I've known you, you've been completely honest with me.'

Before their brief, torrid affair he'd made it clear there would be no future for them, and she'd welcomed that unsparing honesty because it had eased her conscience.

Heat curled her toes as memories flooded back—not ones she wanted to relive now.

She stumbled over her next words before saying, 'To put it in simplistic terms, you just don't seem to be the sort.' And she held her head high and finished, 'But I still think you're overreacting. You don't need to be married to prove that Chloe is better off with you, whom she knows and loves, than a man she's never met.'

Luke looked at her intent face, the fathomless eyes a mysterious mixture of blue and green, and wondered whether she was telling the truth.

Not that it could be allowed to matter.

Resolution hardened within him. Chloe was too important, too vulnerable for him to allow Iona's natural fears to change his mind. His legal advisor had stressed that the best way of making sure his father didn't get his hands on the child would be for Lukas to front up with a wife—one who adored Chloe.

If he were superstitious he'd be tempted to believe

that the gods had been kind to him, sending Iona his way for just this reason. As it was, he was prepared to use whatever bait he could find to persuade her to marry him.

'Probably plenty of seducers have been good with children,' he said cynically. 'However, I am honoured by your trust.'

'Exactly how did you come to adopt Chloe?' she asked quietly.

He paused, then shrugged. 'I was contacted by my father's discarded mistress, frantic because she was pregnant. She told me my father refused to believe it was his child, and although she didn't want the baby, some scruple forbade her to take the obvious way out.' Also, she had seen the child as a bargaining chip, an asset that could be cashed in. 'When I offered her enough money she happily signed the papers for me to adopt the baby.'

Iona said blankly, 'You mean she *sold* Chloe to you?'

'Yes.'

Her face revealed her shock and dismay, and then she asked a question that reinforced his conviction she'd make Chloe an excellent mother. 'Why did you buy her?'

'Because she is my sister,' he said honestly. 'I had her DNA tested when she was born, of course.'

'Of course,' she said on a spurt of irritation.

Luke almost smiled, but this was too important. The fact that he'd had her investigated clearly still stung. Besides, she'd done her own checking; she certainly already knew of the sordid reason for his father's disinheritance. 'I am Greek, Iona, the only son. I was brought

up to believe that the family was my responsibility—and
that means everyone in it.'

'What about your father?'

He shrugged. 'I am no longer his son.'

'How did he find out Chloe was his daughter?'

She had the right to know.

Concisely, Lukas replied, 'The woman who gave
birth to Chloe has run through the money I paid her.
She approached me for more and I refused to give her
any. My initial payment to her should have been enough
to support her for the rest of her life, but she has wasted
it away. So out of spite she went to my father and told
him what she'd done. Possibly he paid her well for the
information—I neither know nor care.'

Iona glanced at him, her mysterious mermaid's eyes
troubled. 'Why does he believe her now?'

'I don't know whether he did believe her,' Luke said
curtly. His father simply hadn't been prepared to pass
up a possible opportunity to attack him. 'However, she
must have been convincing enough for him to obtain
a sample of Chloe's DNA—bribe a chambermaid at a
hotel we've stayed at, possibly—and have it tested.' He
glanced at the documents he'd unpacked, and then back
at Iona. 'The results show conclusively that she is his
true daughter.'

Her brow wrinkled. 'But you adopted her—legally
you are her father, not him. He has no claim to her.'

'Not all countries have legal systems as impeccably
lacking in corruption as yours in New Zealand, and the
fact that he is her birth father is strong support to his
case. My father has power and connections, and the will
to use both. It is important to him to take from me what
he believes is rightfully his.'

Iona felt sick. Scandalised, she blurted, 'She's not a

thing—to be bought and sold with no concern for her feelings. I wouldn't do that to a pet, let alone a child.'

'Good,' Luke said calmly. 'I thought as much. I'll set the wheels in motion for a quick wedding. I believe Tahiti has just established a residency period of three days, so we'll go back there.'

Her shock chilling into an unbearable mixture of panic and betraying anticipation, Iona scanned his uncompromising face.

She was being torn in two, her new-found love warring with a profound caution warning of heart-wrenching danger. To live unloved—to marry a man who saw her as someone who'd help him win a legal case... 'I haven't agreed to that! Why is it so necessary for you to marry someone?'

'Not *someone*—you.' He paused deliberately. 'If you were making a decision about the welfare of a three-year-old, which father would you choose—a bachelor who travels a lot, or a man happily married to a wife who is fond of the child?'

Chilled, she said stubbornly, 'If they loved her either would be better than a total stranger like your father.'

'I will do whatever I have to retain custody,' he said inflexibly, 'and I have a much better chance of achieving that if I show that Chloe is happy in a stable family situation. She loves Neelie, and her nanny loves her, but Neelie is old school and not comfortable with displays of affection. Even in these few short days you have given Chloe something Neelie never could—fun and vitality and youth. She already relies on you, and is learning to love you. You might not love her yet, but it won't take long.'

Iona opened her mouth, then closed it again. She

didn't dare admit that leaving Chloe would be a huge wrench.

His brows lifted, but when she remained resolutely silent he went on, 'If I can prove I'm giving Chloe a settled home life, with two people she loves and who love her—as opposed to life with an old man who has never seen her and a nanny who will also be a total stranger—my legal team tell me it will make an important difference.'

But what about me? Iona thought cravenly. Torn by a mixture of temptation and stark fear at his cold-blooded summation of the situation, she chewed on her lip, only stopping when his gaze came to rest on her maltreated mouth and a spark lit the tawny depths of his eyes.

'Don't do that,' he said imperiously.

His intent gaze set need smouldering into life, tightening her skin and setting her nerves alight.

Only to be quenched when he went on, 'And, as the only man in the family, I will, of course, make sure your cousin and her sons are cared for.'

'Don't try that—you can't buy Angie,' she flashed. 'Or me, if it comes to that.'

'I'm not trying to buy either of you,' he said evenly, but his eyes narrowed. Holding her gaze, he drawled, 'And if I were to *try* anything with you, it would be seduction.'

His smile sent hot little rills of anticipation through Iona. Colour swept up, heating her skin, only to fade, leaving her cold and uncertain when he spoke again.

'But that is not my intention. This is too important for cheap tricks. Chloe's future depends on integrity from both of us.'

Relief swept over Iona—followed almost immediately by aching disappointment. Some weak part of her wished he'd dazzle her into taking this step into the unknown instead of logically—honestly—setting out his reasons for needing a wife.

A temporary wife at that, she suspected. And the stark chill of that thought numbed her into silence.

CHAPTER EIGHT

'As I told you before,' Luke said, 'I was bred to take my place as head of the family—it is part of what I am. By marrying me you will become my responsibility, and so will your cousin and her boys.' His expression iced into contempt. 'Especially since their father doesn't take an interest in them, and they apparently have no other relatives except you.'

Iona felt the jaws of a trap closing around her. A trap made of her love for both the man and the child. Panic tightened her nerves. 'I suppose you found that out when you had me investigated?' she snapped.

'Relatives have to be taken into consideration when I'm choosing a nanny for Chloe,' he said, equally blunt. 'Now, give me an answer.'

Thoughts jostling chaotically, feeling herself backed into a corner, Iona put off a reply by asking, 'If I refuse, what will you do?'

'Persuade you,' he said promptly, and smiled at her.

He didn't move, but she felt the power and intensity of his will, fierce and compelling, backed by the force of his personality.

His voice deepened into a lazy caress. 'Would it be so difficult, Iona? We are good together—you can't deny that. For me there has never been another woman like you. Is it the same for you?'

'Yes,' she said, dazzled into foolishness, then could have cut her tongue out. She'd handed him an overwhelming advantage.

Ruthlessly he used it. 'So would it be so difficult to become my wife? We could have a good life together, you and I.'

Temptation clouded her mind with honeyed urging; she didn't dare look at him because she could feel her defiance seeping away. She should be angry for even considering his outrageous proposal—no, not a proposal, she reminded herself, he'd called it a proposition.

Thoughts jostled feverishly in her mind. Denied of his family, Luke had built himself another. If his father succeeded in destroying that, she would always feel responsible. Luke loved the child he'd adopted; if he lost her something hugely important would be taken from him.

It would be a measure of Iona's love if she did this for him.

When she spoke her voice sounded oddly disconnected. 'And how long do you expect this marriage to last?'

'For as long as you want it.'

She said desperately, 'Luke, it wouldn't work. We don't even know each other—not really.'

His lashes drooped, hiding his thoughts as he covered the floor between them in several strides. He stopped, close enough to tease her nostrils with the faint, fresh tang that was his alone. A surge of white-hot sensation—raw and sinfully enticing—locked Iona's breath in her throat and sent her thoughts stumbling into confusion again.

His textured voice warm with amusement, backed by something more primal—a distinctly territorial note—he said, 'Now you're scraping the bottom of the barrel. We have slept in each other's arms night after night, made love with unconfined passion, laughed together, played together. I know you make love like some ancient goddess, and that your delicious sensuality is reinforced by genuine honesty, a warm heart and a good mind. Of course we know each other. I know you are growing fond of Chloe. And you did not doubt that I was innocent of the accusations of my father's wife.'

Every nerve quivering with the restraint she enforced, she said unevenly, 'But it wasn't anything more than a holiday romance. You made no attempt to get in touch with me afterwards.'

'You hoped I would?'

'No.' It was almost the truth; her guilt over what she'd seen as the betrayal of her love for Gavin had made her feel she didn't want anything to do with Luke. But the time she'd spent with him had laid the foundations for her to think more clearly, and the guilt had dissipated.

Now she wondered what she'd have done if he had contacted her.

She saw his chest lift as he took in a breath. 'The day you left my father took another step in the never-ending war he conducts with me. I had to fight on several fronts; it took me some time to block him. And then Chloe got meningitis.'

She gasped, and he nodded. 'It was a difficult time. And I didn't know if you had got over your love for your fiancé. But I never thought it was simply a holiday fling—surely you understood that when I asked you to go with me?'

'You didn't intend permanence,' she said slowly,

her body insensibly warming. His closeness was a threat, undermining the part of her brain that warned her no joy could possibly come of a marriage based on practicality.

And sex, she thought practically. Marvellous sex. Surely as their lives knitted together her love would be enough to make a success of any marriage?

'I didn't,' he admitted. 'But I did intend us to get to know each other—out of bed,' he said on a low laugh, and took her in his arms, pulling her so close she could feel the taut strength in his body.

'This is not going to help,' she managed to mutter, before his grip tightened even further so that every honed sense leapt into full awareness.

His mouth found hers and took it in a kiss so disturbingly sensual she forgot everything in the wonder of it.

Until he lifted his head and looked down at her with intent, gleaming eyes.

Unbearably stimulated, she shakily blurted the first thought that came to her from the maelstrom of her mind. 'I thought you said you weren't going to try seduction.'

His lashes drooped, hiding his satisfaction. 'That can wait. But I intend this to be a real marriage,' he said calmly as he released her and stepped back. 'I am not of the temperament to stay celibate, and when I remember how it was for us both in Tahiti I think that you'll agree it would be unnecessarily foolish of us to even consider such a thing. Besides, I would like more children; Chloe needs brothers and sisters.'

Iona's heart jumped in her breast. The sensations still churning through her blocked any coherent thought process; she wanted to tell him that the whole situation was outrageously impossible, but some treacherous part of her kept reminding her of new-found love, of the passionate eroticism of those nights and days in Tahiti.

Mingled with the memories were fears for Chloe, possibly to be taken from the man she considered to be her father and handed over to an old, bitter, angry stranger who viewed her as a weapon. It would be a devastating blow for the child.

A knock on the door made her start. Luke frowned and said, 'Leave it.'

'I'll go to my room. I need time to think,' she said swiftly.

He fixed her with a keen glance, but didn't object. However, when she turned to go he commanded, 'Stay a moment. If this is what I suspect it is, you should know about it.'

Puzzled, she watched him take delivery of a courier parcel. He signed a receipt, waited until the courier had gone, then slit open the package.

The contents were documents. Luke flicked through them, his face impassive, and then dropped them onto the nearest table as though they contaminated him.

'My father,' he said shortly. 'To tell me he is sending a nanny to pick up his daughter.'

Appalled, Iona stared at him. 'Surely he doesn't expect you to just hand her over? She's lived with you for three years...'

Her voice trailed away at the smile that hardened his face. Cold and satirical, it chilled her blood.

'He knows I will not do that without a fight,' he stated. 'Apparently Chloe's mother is now willing to state on oath that I forced her to allow me to adopt. That almost guarantees a very nasty legal case that could drag on for years.'

'How could they do that?' Iona asked numbly. 'Can't they see what such a case would do to Chloe? Don't they care about her at all?'

Luke said cynically, 'Chloe's mother wants money so that she can indulge herself; my father wants only to assert power over me. Chloe means nothing to them except a way of achieving what they want.'

Closing her eyes, Iona fought back a deep sense of foreboding. There was no longer a choice; she could not do that to the child. She'd seen the damage done to Angie's children by a father who'd abandoned them, and there had been others in the nursery school—children without roots, already showing signs of disturbance.

If it was possible to save Chloe from such a fate, she had to do what she could. But first she had to face the final hurdle—one even her love wouldn't be able to overcome.

She took a deep breath and said thinly, 'All right. I'll marry you. But *I* want something too.'

'I understand,' Luke said cynically. 'What is it?'

Holding her head high, she met eyes of burnished gold, searching and unreadable. 'Your promise that you'll be faithful.'

When he said nothing she braced herself. If he wouldn't give on this, she wouldn't—*couldn't*—agree to marry him. A union of one-sided love was bad enough; one where she'd be faced with his adultery was impossible. It would kill her.

No muscle moved in his face. 'Of course.'

'I don't think there's any *of course* about it,' she said, her tone matching his expression. 'I happen to despise people who break their vows.'

Luke said quietly, 'I too. I will do my best to make sure that you never regret your decision.'

His grave, oddly formal statement wasn't what she wanted, but she trusted him to keep his promise, and her hopeful heart dreamed that the attraction he felt might some day turn to love.

So she ignored the pang of useless disappointment to ask, 'In that case, what happens now?'

In an oddly taut voice he said, 'We will fly to Tahiti as soon as possible. Knowledge of our previous affair there will establish a history for us. It might help convince a judge that our marriage is not a deliberate attempt to forestall my father's claim to Chloe.'

No sentimentality there. Feeling empty, as though he'd dashed some forbidden hope, she said, 'I'm still finding it almost impossible to believe he has any chance of success.'

Luke shrugged. 'I hope you are right. However I don't want her life overshadowed by years of legal wrangling. It is possible that when he realises he is fighting a good marriage and a devoted pair of parents with a happy child he might give this up without going so far as taking us to court.'

'Possible, but not probable?' she guessed.

He gave a sardonic smile. 'I see you understand. Do you have a ring that fits you?'

Iona glanced down at her hands. 'Not here.'

Gavin's engagement ring still nestled in a drawer at home, but it was hardly appropriate.

Luke said crisply, 'Then we need string to measure the size of your ring finger.'

Iona's fingers curled into her palms. She forced herself to relax, unclenching both fists at her sides. Gavin's memory had faded into the past, relinquished without pain, but a residual guilt hurt her for a moment. So many times she'd said goodbye to him; this would be the last.

Uncannily, Luke said, 'He is dead, Iona.'

She went white. 'How…how did you know what I was thinking?' she whispered.

'A certain look—a shadow across your face.' He shrugged, a typical brief lift of his shoulders. 'He was a good man, and you would have been happy with him, but he is long dead. Let him go in peace.'

'I have. It's just that the last time my finger size was taken was for his engagement ring,' she said quietly, and gave him the measurement, adding, 'He's gone from my life, Luke.' And, because it had to be said, she added with a shaky smile, 'He left when I met you.'

'Good.' He held out his hand, and reluctantly she put hers into it.

In a strange way that simple handclasp was more intimate than the kiss they'd just exchanged. Lean, long fingers closed around hers so firmly she tensed, but before the grip tightened into pain they eased. Yet it felt as though Luke was establishing some sort of claim on her—a claim he reinforced by lifting her hand to kiss the back of her fingers, then turned it and kissed her wrist.

With the touch of his mouth lingering on her skin, she thought he was gentling her into acceptance, forging a connection between them that transformed their purely physical previous one.

He looked down and said, 'You have lovely hands, as graceful as they are capable. We'll fly back to Auckland tonight and I'll organise a ring fitting for you at the apartment. If there's nothing you like we can wait until we reach Tahiti—they have an excellent selection of pearls there, some of which are as changeable as your eyes.'

But that evening she picked a tourmaline so blazingly blue it reminded her of the lagoon in Tahiti. On either side of the stone diamonds blazed in platinum.

Approvingly, the jeweller said, 'A superb choice. The stone comes from Brazil, and this colour is so valued that a perfect gem like this is more precious than a diamond of the same quality.' She glanced up at Iona and added, 'It matches your eyes.'

'Just now, perhaps.' Iona smiled. 'They tend to change shades when I wear different coloured clothes.'

'They are beautiful,' Luke said. He nodded at the ring. 'And so is that. Leave it here, thank you.'

He saw the jeweller out and came silently back. Iona hadn't moved. She was still standing a few feet away from the window, staring at the ring as if it were a snake. For a moment compunction struck him; he banished it. He would make her a good husband, and he couldn't allow himself to feel anything but relief that Chloe now had a much better chance of a happy childhood and adolescence.

He picked up the ring. 'Come here,' he said softly.

Shadowed eyes shifting between a deep blue and a fathomless green, she said huskily, 'Why?'

'Because I want to give you this ring.'

All expression vanished from her face. 'Nothing's stopping you.'

He wondered just what was going on behind that calm face, that mysterious gaze. She was a challenge; the only things he really knew about her was that she didn't want to marry him, and that she made love like a siren.

No, he knew much more; she was also tender-hearted

enough to be manipulated by affection for a child. He started towards her and saw a quick flush heat the skin along her cheekbones. Hunger tore at him like a whirlwind, eating at the control he'd been forced to exercise since he'd received the first parcel of legal papers from his lawyers.

It would be easy enough to forget his cold anger at his father in wild sex, but now was not the time. Iona was prepared to sacrifice her life for Chloe; he would give her the knowledge that he respected her as well as wanted her. He could wait until their marriage to take her to bed.

He stopped in front of her, saw the colour come and go in her skin, and lifted her left hand. Frowning a little, he slid the ring onto her finger. It slipped easily enough at first, but had to be eased past the second knuckle.

Iona stiffened, then watched lean tanned fingers settle it into place. The silvery circle felt cold and heavy, but it was swiftly warmed by the blood pumping through her body, the burgeoning heat of her response to Luke's closeness.

Kiss me, her mind pleaded, so importunately she wondered if she'd actually said the words out loud.

No, thank heavens.

And Luke didn't kiss her. In a gesture that made her shiver, he raised her hand and kissed the ring, then pressed his mouth into her palm, before folding her fingers over his kiss.

Her breath came short through her lips.

He said quietly, 'I shall never be able to thank you enough for this.'

Don't thank me, she thought frantically, unable to read anything in the arrogantly handsome face, the steady golden glint of his eyes.

Don't thank me, love me...

Words she couldn't say.

No, that was defeatist; perhaps one day she could whisper them to him.

One day, when she was confident he'd say them back.

Luke dropped her hand. 'Because of the international dateline we will arrive in Tahiti only an hour or so behind New Zealand time, so neither Chloe nor you should have too much difficulty adjusting your body clocks.'

'I hope not,' Iona said. 'It's only a few days since she went through the process in Auckland.'

He said calmly, 'She is remarkably adaptable.'

Because she'd had to be, travelling with him. Iona realised she had no idea of the sort of life he intended for them. She asked, 'Do you plan to have us travel with you when...from now on?'

'Once we are married?' he said, his voice hard. 'You can say it, Iona; it is not a death sentence or a deed so foul it can't be mentioned.'

She flushed, but said spiritedly, 'I'm still getting used to the idea! If you insist on bulldozing your way into people's lives you have to expect them to be shell-shocked for a few days!'

Brows drawing together, he stared at her—and then to her astonishment he threw his head back and laughed.

'I see all of us will have adjustments to make,' he said dryly, 'and not just to various time zones. Yes, whenever it's possible—certainly while Chloe is not at school— you will travel with me.'

She looked up to find his eyes on her, unexpectedly keen. 'It's good for a child to have a settled base.'

Luke said, 'So people have said. I don't think she's missing anything.'

'That's because to Chloe you are her home.'

He said sombrely, 'Yes. However, until we know her future, it will be politic to lead a less peripatetic life. I have a house in London, and apartments in New York and Athens as well as the beach house in Tahiti, but the place I call home is an island south of Greece. Once we are married I intend to spend more time there. Will you be bored on a Greek island?'

Not when you're there, she thought with an inward tremor. 'I doubt it. I usually find plenty to do. I'll want to learn Greek, and I have a degree to finish.'

'A degree? In what?'

'Early childhood education,' she told him.

His expression softened into a smile. 'Excellent—I learn new things about you all the time. Will you be able to finish it from half the world away?'

'I'll find out. Don't worry about me, Luke. I'm adaptable.'

The next few days passed in a blur. When Luke made up his mind, Iona realised, things happened—fast. He even managed to dazzle Angie into acceptance of the situation. It took a considerable expenditure of his effortless charm, but nowhere near as much as Iona had expected.

After a very early start Luke's private jet landed in Tahiti in the heat of a tropical noon, to the scent of flowers and the mingled sound of singing and the sea, and the stunning physical beauty of the people.

Even in that hothouse atmosphere Luke garnered more than his share of attention, with women eyeing him with open appreciation before transferring envious gazes to Iona. Aware of her chainstore clothes, she felt an unusual sense of inferiority; she couldn't compete with these women in the brilliantly hued swathes of cloth they called a *pareu*, women who wore flowers in their long, glossily dark tresses with an insouciance she'd never be able to match.

And that she was even thinking in terms of competition made her angry with herself. Somehow being with Luke had turned her into a different woman, one with a disheartening lack of confidence.

They took a boat across the lagoon to the palm-fringed beach where they'd met, walking beneath the palms and through a garden perfumed by more flowers. Vivid and gaudy, they looked exquisitely at home.

'Pretty,' Chloe said with satisfaction, touching the silken petals of a scarlet hibiscus. However, when she sniffed the long pollen-laden centre stamen she quickly released it and looked disappointed.

'Try this,' Iona suggested, snapping off a bloom from the native gardenia.

Chloe sniffed the fragrant white flower, and beamed. 'Nice,' she announced, and held it out to Luke, who stopped and inhaled the scent.

'Better than any perfume in a bottle,' he pronounced, and tucked it behind the child's ear, smiling down at her. 'It is called *tiare tahiti*,' he told her, 'and the Tahitians use it for garlands. When Iona and I get married we will both wear a garland made of *tiare* flowers, because they are the wedding flowers for Tahiti.'

Her face crinkled against the sun. 'Will I have one too?' she asked.

Luke glanced across at Iona, who nodded, for the first time feeling she had a part to play in the arrangements.

'Of course, if you wish to wear one,' he said.

'I do,' Chloe said fervently, transferring her wide beam from him to Iona.

Cradling the blossom in place in her long dark hair, she tucked her other little paw into Luke's big hand as they walked the rest of the way, ending at the house Iona remembered so well. There they were enthusiastically welcomed by the caretaker, a short man of French extraction, and his tall, serious-faced wife who acted as housekeeper.

'Moana and Jacques you remember, I'm sure,' Luke said.

'Of course I do.' She smiled at them both, and went off with the housekeeper to settle Chloe in.

For Iona the day was clouded by a pang of…not envy, not even regret, an emotion more shadowy and fragile than either.

Last time she'd been here it had been as Luke's temporary lover.

CHAPTER NINE

THINGS were so different now, although the sun still beamed down in a languorous caress. Desire uncoiled in supplication, summoning heated, erotic memories that tightened every nerve in delicious anticipation.

Cut that out, Iona ordered her body. Face facts—especially when they're terrifying.

This time she loved Luke. And she'd promised to marry him. Her stomach hollowed out as though in anticipation of a blow. How was she was going to cope with marriage to a man who saw her as nothing more than a necessary evil?

Don't overdramatise, she commanded, trying to ignore a swift flash of desolation. Emotions were all very well, but they needed to be reined in by logic and reason. She didn't really believe Luke thought of her as an evil.

A frisson of sensation sizzled through her when she recalled the glint of heat in his eyes whenever he looked at her. But a lot of men found it quite easy to have sex with a woman they didn't necessarily like much. Did Luke see her as a pawn to be manipulated for his own—and Chloe's—ends?

Possibly. If she were in his position she'd probably feel the same—the welfare of her child taking paramount place. Whereas she felt much, much more than that for him—and not just because of his potent physical presence, either, or memories of his superb talent as a lover.

She stood on the terrace, eyeing Luke's powerful back, the lean strength of his torso set above long, muscled legs, the purposeful grace of his movements as he moderated his steps to fit Chloe's little trot.

How had his father's rejection affected him? Had he been a spoilt young man, taking his position as the adored only son and heir for granted? Aristo Michelakis's refusal to accept his word had bitten deep, and being thrown out of his family must have scarred some essential part of his soul.

He'd certainly set out to prove himself, and succeeded brilliantly. His reputation as a businessman was legendary and the speed of his rise in that cut-throat world had taken it by surprise.

He'd even made a new family for himself. And succeeded there too; Chloe bore all the hallmarks of a child secure in the knowledge she was loved.

Discovering he'd spent the first year of Chloe's life caring for her himself might have been the tipping point, the hidden moment when Iona had crossed the border from desire to love. His affection for the child had touched an unknown hunger in her, and before she'd realised it—with no effort on his part—she'd let down her barricades. Somehow that unrecognised surrender had helped transform a powerful physical desire into love.

She was certainly nothing like the woman who'd once walked along this beach convinced she'd never feel again, that she was doomed to a grey existence of no emotion, separated from the rest of life by a veil of despair.

Luke, with his open and genuine appreciation of her as a sensual, desirable woman, had torn that veil into shreds, reuniting her with the world.

Would she have agreed to marry him if she hadn't loved him?

It was a question she couldn't answer.

But the decision was irrevocable. Not only did she love Luke, but in this short time Chloe too had wound her way into her heart; it wasn't just for Luke's sake that she'd do whatever had to be done to keep the little girl secure.

'Look, Miss Iona,' Chloe said importantly, running up to her, a shell in one little hand. 'I found it on the beach.'

Without looking at Luke, Iona said, 'Chloe, how would you like to call me Iona?'

'Can I really?' Chloe beamed, then lifted her face to Luke, seeking confirmation.

He nodded. 'A good idea,' he said, his gaze warm as he smiled at Iona.

Whose heart somersaulted in her chest. 'Let's go and wash it in our bathroom,' she said.

Again her room was right beside Chloe's—something that startled and disappointed her, because presumably Moana had followed Luke's orders. The placement made a definite statement about the reason she was there—to take care of Chloe.

As she unpacked she indulged in a gloomy vision of being left behind on some Greek island while Luke zoomed around the world, of loveless sex for the sole attempt to conceive those children Luke said he wanted, of his eventual terminal boredom with her...

Too late now, she thought wearily as tension closed its claws on her. And she was overdramatising again—a habit that seemed to have crept up on her since Luke had re-entered her life.

She glanced out of the glass doors with their shutters pushed back. The small terrace outside served the two bedrooms; furniture beckoned, and the scent of the sea mingled with that of the flowering shrubs. Sunlight sifted down through the fronds of palms, casting shifting shadows that looked like a pattern of textiles. Through curving grey trunks the lagoon glimmered, an intense colour that echoed the sky.

At least she'd have a variety of beautiful places to be miserable in…

Snap out of it, she told herself abruptly. Luke wanted her—he couldn't hide that. She'd have to learn to be content with what she had, and hope that his desire would one day grow into real love. Setting her jaw, she went into Chloe's room and her unpacked her clothes, the child's chattering lifting her mood.

Luke was called away to the telephone, so she took Chloe down to the lagoon and splashed in the warm, silken water, overseen by a Tahitian man with the same watchful, silent air of competence as Iakobos, who'd left them at Auckland airport.

They ate lunch together with no sign of Luke, and then Iona settled Chloe down for a nap. She saw nothing more of Luke until it was time for him to read to Chloe before she went to sleep.

Over dinner Luke said, 'I am sorry I had to spend the day working. Something came up that needed my attention.'

A note in his voice warned her the *something* hadn't been welcome. 'All well now?'

He shrugged. 'I have done what I could,' he said briefly before abruptly changing the subject. 'Our wedding will be held on the beach here; it will be a ceremony with traditional Tahitian features. I hope you do not mind that?'

The already familiar mixture of excitement and apprehension roiled through Iona. 'What exactly will it entail?'

'First we will be given Tahitian names, then we will exchange leis of *tiare tahiti* as a symbol of our unity. After that a priest will bless us, and we will be married. There will be singing and dancing, of course. Like Greeks, the Tahitians accompany all of life's great moments and most of its lesser ones with both.'

'It sounds lovely and informal,' she said cautiously.

His smile held more than a hint of irony. 'I hope you will enjoy it. Angie and the boys certainly should.'

Iona said, 'Thank you for flying them over.'

'Naturally you will want them here,' he said dismissively. He paused, then said, 'Did Chloe speak to you about being a flower girl?'

'No,' she said, with a glance towards Chloe's room. 'I told her I'd ask.'

Remorsefully she said, 'I should have thought of that myself. I'd love to have her as a flower girl, but where can we get her a frock?'

She'd chosen her own wedding dress in a boutique in Auckland, taking far too long selecting a creation that virtually emptied her bank account. Fortunately she already owned a pair of sandals that would look great with it, and for flowers she wanted nothing more than a wreath of gardenias for her hair and a small posy to carry, both of which had been organised.

When she'd arrived back at the penthouse Luke had

looked up from the game he was playing with Chloe, and casually asked for the details of her bank account.

'Why?' she'd responded, a little curtly.

He'd sighed heavily as Chloe gleefully shouted, 'Go Fish!'

'I think you can see through the cards,' he complained, widening Chloe's grin. He picked up the card and went on in the tone he used to indicate to Chloe that there was no negotiation. 'I shall make you a monthly allowance.'

Iona stiffened, but he said reasonably, 'It is either that or you'll have to come running to me whenever you want to buy a packet of chewing gum.'

'I don't chew gum,' she pointed out.

'Toothpaste, then.' His smile summoned a reluctant one from her. 'You'll want a reasonably large sum at first for clothes and other things. Afterwards we can discuss a monthly amount.'

Of course it was sensible. She thought now of the indecently large amount that had appeared in her account and told herself it was ridiculously missish to feel as though she'd been bought.

Luke said, 'Tomorrow morning a woman from Papeete will come across with a selection of suitable outfits for Chloe. And perhaps I should warn you that our daughter has very definite ideas about her clothes.'

Our daughter… His words kindled a warmth in Iona's heart.

While they'd been eating dusk had swooped in from the sea, turning the island into a magical place of moonlight and shadows, of scents that became more potent and evocative after the sun went down. The thickening atmosphere almost silenced the ever-present whispering of the trade winds in the coconut palms, and far out to sea a bird called—a faint, solitary sound that echoed Iona's fey mood exactly.

She wanted—oh, she wanted Luke...

Couldn't he sense she longed for him to sweep her off her feet, to banish every doubt and fear with passion, convince her with fierce lovemaking that she'd made the right decision?

Instead he seemed determined to stay detached and practical. The splendid moulding of his face revealed no emotion; he looked at her with cool golden eyes, and all through the day he'd treated her with the sort of neutral, impersonal courtesy that forbade any emotional response.

They could be entering on a business partnership, she thought dismally.

Actually, that's almost certainly how he saw it.

Unless he too was wondering if he'd made the wrong decision—if tying himself to a woman he didn't love would doom him to a life of barren emotions and sex.

Somehow she knew he'd keep the promises he'd made to her, but here in lush Tahiti that knowledge was no consolation. She didn't want him chained to her by his sense of honour.

Coolly, he said, 'I hope you're not considering a change of mind, Iona.'

Startled, she looked across the table to him. His relentless gaze roamed her face, and then he smiled, a humourless movement of his lips.

'I thought as much,' he said, and got to his feet.

Eyes widening, she watched him stride around the table. Even in a casual shirt with a lavalava swathed around his narrow hips, he projected an air of effortless intimidation.

A reckless hope surged through her, sweeping away common sense in a few wild, nerve-racking seconds.

He said objectively, 'It's called pre-wedding nerves, and I have been best man at enough weddings to know that it affects both sexes.'

How could he be so *reasonable*?

Coming to a stop behind her, he rested his hands on her bare shoulders. Only a few moments before she'd been longing for him to touch her; now it was not enough. The sensation of those long, tanned fingers against her pale skin dried her mouth and smoked through her brain, rendering her almost witless.

'It would have been better if we could have had a week or so by ourselves, so that we could get reacquainted,' he said, still in that pleasant, level tone. 'At least by marrying here we won't be faced with a media circus. No one knows we are here, and even if they do they certainly won't know our plans.'

Iona blinked. 'I doubt that very much,' she said trying to match his level tone. 'News travels very fast in the Pacific. By the time we've established residency I imagine everyone who's interested will know exactly why we're here.'

The tension within her was spiralling out of control, but she managed to stay still, soaking up pleasure from his nearness and the steady warmth of his hands.

Yearning softened her mouth, brought a flush to her skin. Surely he could feel it heating beneath his fingers?

And then he said, 'You must be tired. And I unfortunately have this—situation to deal with. So I shall say goodnight.'

But before he moved away he stooped and brushed his lips across the nape of her neck. Every tiny invisible hair on her skin stood upright at that lightest of touches and she stopped breathing as a tide of delight filled her.

Without volition she turned and lifted her face. Stone-faced, he looked down at her and she held her breath, and then he said in a harsh voice, 'I cannot stay.'

'I know.'

Tension wound between them. His eyes kindled and he muttered, 'You are too tempting, and I must go...'

His mouth came down on hers in a kiss that ended far too soon. He lifted his head and put her from him, and without a backwards look strode from the room.

It was little enough to dream on, that swift kiss, but it comforted her as much as it frustrated her.

The next morning Luke was closeted with a telephone until after lunch. From her seat beneath the big tree that shaded the terrace, Iona looked up from her book. His face was drawn, the strong framework emphasised.

'Everything all right?' she asked tentatively.

He shrugged, as though easing out kinks in his shoulders. 'As far as it can be.' He paused, then said, 'A family matter.'

She frowned. 'I thought—I thought you had no contact with your family.'

'That is so. A young cousin rang me—we have not met since I left home, but she was distraught and I was her last hope. Her parents have been trying to push her into a marriage she does not want—her father's business is going under, and the groom-to-be is prepared to help. My father thinks it will be a good alliance, so she has no help there. To be fair to Aristo he has bailed them out several times before—my uncle is not a good businessman. So my cousin was reduced to calling on me.'

'What did you do?'

He gave a brief, mirthless smile. 'It took a little time, but I managed to persuade her parents that saving the family business was not worth their daughter's happiness.'

Indignation burnt through her. This was the family who'd accepted his father's version of events and cut him out of their lives. Without thinking she got up and went to him, putting a hand on his arm. Every muscle was flexed and taut. 'In other words, you bailed them out?'

He looked down with hard, unreadable eyes. 'Of course. She was a charming child, and she has always wanted to become a doctor.'

Iona said quietly, 'They don't deserve your help.'

He smiled, and cupped a cheek with one hand, eyes warming as he looked down at her. Anticipation soared, but almost immediately he stepped back and said, 'My uncle did not enjoy the conditions, but his desperate situation means he has no option. Enough of them—they are not important. It's unlikely we'll hear from them again. I have some unsettling news about our wedding.'

A cold pool of foreboding opened up under Iona's ribs. She said, 'You've discovered that you haven't quite divorced your fifth wife?'

His brows shot up, followed by a shout of laughter. 'I'm not so careless,' he said dryly. 'You need have no fear that any discarded woman will cast a shadow over our union. No, it is just that before we have our charming beach wedding we need to marry in a civil ceremony at the office of the local mayor, in what passes for the city hall here.'

'Of course—Tahiti is a French territory. So why is that unsettling?'

'Because the media are already gathering.'

Frowning, Iona chewed at her lip.

He said, 'Don't *do* that! It pains me to see you mal-treating your soft mouth.'

Thrilling at his hot, thick voice, she said, 'You sound like my mother.'

'I doubt it,' he said roughly, and the air between them was suddenly charged with an intensity that tightened every nerve in Iona's body.

'I'll try to stop myself, but apparently it's always been a habit of mine.' Her voice emerged oddly off-key, and she went on hurriedly, 'I'm not...I've never had to deal with the media.'

'You will not deal with it,' he said instantly. 'I shall put out a press release as soon as we are married, but it wouldn't surprise me if we have to run some sort of gauntlet. It seems word has somehow got out that my father is suing for custody.' He ignored Iona's shocked dismay. 'Which means we will leave Chloe here when we go for that first ceremony; I will not have her worried by any questions. And the security will have to be increased.'

Iona didn't blame him for being thoroughly fed up; this new development, combined with the pressure of the family situation, was enough to erode the control of any man, even one as accustomed to pressure as Luke.

She turned as he said something in Greek. Eyes narrowed, he was looking across the silken, empty sands of the beach to the aquamarine depths of the lagoon, placid and devoid of any activity except for a canoe edging in towards the beach.

Following his gaze, Iona saw two men appear briefly

from the coconut palms that bordered the sand. One spoke into some sort of communications device while the other strode down to meet the craft and the three men in it.

'Journalists?' she ventured.

'Probably,' he returned austerely, switching his gaze to her face. 'I will make sure this fuss affects you as little as possible, even if I have to blanket the island with security men.'

A couple of expert swishes of the paddle from the oarsman in the canoe had it backing away from the beach, but Iona saw a man in a loud Hawaiian shirt lift a camera and take several shots of the house.

The downside of power and privilege, she thought, the chill hollow beneath her ribs expanding. And this would be her life...

'Don't look so worried,' Luke said crisply. He came towards her and took her hands, lifting them to his lips for a lingering second.

His heavy-lidded eyes gleamed with a golden promise—a promise extinguished too soon when he said, 'That should provide them with a photograph romantic enough to show we're lovers.'

Although the last thing Iona wanted was an embrace then, she had to fight a bitter spasm of disappointment when he released her.

Almost offhandedly he said, 'Most of the time the only media interested in me are reporters for the financial columns. If it weren't for the custody case our wedding would have been the quiet affair we both want.'

'Do you think your father released the information to the press?' she asked, appalled.

Thin-lipped, he said, 'It seems likely. Forget about him. On my island in Greece we will have complete freedom; everyone has known me since I was born, and while they are interested, as everyone there is in all their neighbours, they would not dream of intruding—just as I would not intrude in their lives.'

Iona wondered if *his* island, as he so tellingly described it, was the one place where he felt truly at home.

She said, 'I can cope with journalists, however intrusive, but I hope your heavies can keep them away from the beach ceremony. I'd hate Chloe to be frightened by any sort of media pack.'

Luke said grimly, 'My men will have it under control.'

'That canoe got close enough a few minutes ago.' When he lifted a brow at her, she said, 'Ah—of course. They were allowed to.'

'You see too much,' he said, with a brief unamused smile. 'No one else will get that close. And we may be overreacting. We are not film stars marrying for the third time, or royalty with jewels to display.'

And I am a complete nobody, she thought wearily, then turned her head when he said, 'Is that Chloe I hear?'

'I don't think so.' But she went to look, only to find her charge slumbering, cheeks flushed, her toy lion hugged to her chest.

Wondering if he'd deliberately changed the subject, Iona turned to slip out again, but, as if realising that someone was watching her, Chloe woke, and smiled sleepily at her before holding out her arms.

Iona's heart expanded. 'Hello, darling,' she said softly, and went across to lift the small warm bundle from the bed. 'Good sleep?'

Chloe buried her face in Iona's shoulder and snuggled,

before yawning prodigiously and rubbing her eyes. 'Can I have a drink?' she asked, before adding seriously, 'Please?'

'Of course you can.' And, because Chloe seemed perfectly content to stay in her arms, Iona carried her through to the kitchen.

Halfway there she met Luke. 'She is too heavy for you,' he said, and took her from Iona's arms, kissing Chloe's cheek before he set her on her feet. 'You must not let Iona carry you,' he told her firmly. 'You are a big girl now, and Iona is not strong enough. See, she is slim like a princess.'

Chloe nodded, but when her mouth trembled Iona interposed, 'Truly, carrying you for short distances won't hurt me at all.'

Luke straightened. 'For short distances only,' he said sternly, adding, 'And Chloe must jump.' He smiled down at his daughter. 'Let's show Iona how we lift you up. One, two, three, *jump*!'

Chloe leapt into the air, was caught by his strong arms, and laughed joyously, holding her face up to be kissed again. Iona watched them with something like envy. Whatever happened she'd never regret adding to this child's security. She already loved her, and to take her away from Luke would cause him as much pain as it would the child.

CHAPTER TEN

THAT evening before dinner Iona changed into a pair of soft aqua trousers, topping them with a camisole the same colour. After a moment's frowning pause in front of the mirror she shook her head.

Nobody could call the camisole tight, but the fabric clung to every soft curve. It was stupid, but she felt self-conscious. She pulled on a floaty polyester tunic in mingled shades of blue and green and critically inspected her reflection again.

'Yes,' she said aloud. She loved that tunic, because it gave her skin a glow and turned her eyes into deep pools the same turquoise as the lagoon.

Of course, she thought with a hint of wistful irony, Luke was accustomed to women who wore designer clothes in exquisite fabrics.

She slid her feet into cork-soled green sandals that gave her an extra inch or so of height, and set her shoulders. Two-year-old chainstore clothes or not, if she wanted to eat she had to leave her room.

The meal was served outside on the long terrace, romantically lit by candles. The food was superb, but afterwards Iona couldn't remember it, only the conversation—she remembered every word of that.

And the way the candlelight flickered on Luke's dark,

arrogant features, playing over the angles and planes so that sometimes he looked like an avenging Zeus, sometimes like a magnificent Apollo, sometimes distant, periodically amused.

And always stimulating—in every sense of the word, she thought wildly, thoughts zooming randomly around her head as her body responded to his vital male physicality.

'Chloe tells me she has the prettiest dress in the whole world,' he said. 'I did suggest she model it for me, but she said I wasn't allowed to see it until the wedding.'

Iona laughed softly. 'She loves it. And she's looking forward so much to Angie's arrival with the boys. I had to explain to her how Angie and I are related.'

'She will enjoy having cousins,' he said calmly, but his eyes had turned cold. 'When my father decided to disinherit me, he made it very clear to both my mother's family and his that anyone who so much as recognised me in the street from then on would immediately suffer the same fate.'

Scandalised anew, she said, 'I don't understand how they could do that—believe the lies and turn their backs on you.'

The chill in his eyes was intensified by a flash of bitter amusement. 'It was convenient for them to do so. At that time he was the one with the power and the money.'

Iona said indignantly, 'And apart from your desperate cousin *no one* has made any effort to get in touch with you since then?'

He laughed, a cynical sound that lifted the hairs on her neck. 'Some have made approaches.'

'And?'

'I ignored them,' he told her crisply. 'I do not

subscribe to the notion of revenge, but I learn—and learn well—each lesson that comes along in my life. I trust only those who earn my trust.'

'Or those whose CVs convince your security men that they're decent citizens,' she teased.

His smile returned, the humour plain. 'I can see that will be cast up at me for ever,' he said with mock resignation. 'Perhaps I have something that will help you forgive me.'

She leaned back in her chair as he got to his feet, and watched him walk away, his effortless masculine grace and power working its usual response in her.

What now?

He went into the house, emerging a few seconds later with a small parcel in his hand. Iona eyed it apprehensively, and that smile curved his lips again.

'It is quite harmless,' he said, and handed it to her. 'Consider it a wedding gift.'

She took it, but a thought caused her to lift a dismayed face to him. 'I haven't got you anything,' she said, appalled.

'You have,' he said calmly, golden eyes warming. 'You are giving me yourself—that is all I want.'

If only he wanted her for herself, not for her usefulness... Iona bent her head to the parcel, fumbling to undo it.

It contained a jeweller's case, sleek and expensively branded in gold. Iona didn't dare look at him; her fingers trembled as she opened it.

A sighing gasp escaped her lips. Inside were pearls, exquisitely matched, perfectly graded, their soft silvery-white sheen draping across her fingers like sensuous drops of moonlight. They made a necklace, and beneath them hung a pendant, a heart-shaped pearl framed in diamonds and platinum.

She said quietly, 'Thank you. It's utterly exquisite.'

'Would you like me to help you put it on?' And when she hesitated he said dryly, 'Perhaps not.'

Iona hesitated only a moment before making up her mind. The hunger that gnawed constantly at her had become a driven thing, demanding, insistent, compelling. In silent answer she handed him the pearls and slid the tunic over her head, dropping it over the back of her chair to stand before him in the camisole and trousers.

His eyes kindled, and that involuntary reaction gave her the courage to say, 'Perhaps you could fasten it for me.'

Her voice sounded oddly throaty. Swept by an unexpected attack of shyness, she turned around and presented the tender nape of her neck to him, her breath catching in her throat while she waited for what seemed an eternity.

But it probably only took a few seconds before she felt the silky glide of the gems from the sea against her skin and heard him say, 'So, turn around and let me see.'

She turned, half hiding her eyes with her lashes.

In a voice that sent little shivers of anticipation through her he murmured, 'Ah, I thought that skin like yours, delicate and translucent, would match the pearls for beauty.'

When she coloured his smile turned feral, almost wolfish, but to her mounting—and bewildered—frustration he took a step back, so he could survey her with half-closed eyes.

From a safer distance, she thought, tantalised

beyond endurance. He wanted her—she could see that he wanted her—so what was preventing him from following through?

Short of blurting, *Take me, I'm yours,* like an ingénue in a melodrama, she couldn't make her need any plainer without humiliating herself. All her fears rushed back, pooling in a cold mass beneath her ribs.

'I'm glad you like it,' he said.

'It's lovely.' Her voice was wooden and before he could see her disappointment she turned and said stiffly, 'Can you undo it, please? I'll wear it when we get married.'

She waited, and felt her skin prickle at the light touch of his fingers as he unclasped the necklace.

And then he said in a tense, goaded voice, 'I shall look forward to that. But at the moment all I can think of is making love to you while you are wearing it—and nothing else.'

So what's stopping you?

She turned her head to look up into a face drawn and dark with hunger. Her breath came quick and fierce, her temperature soared into the stratosphere, and the keen desire became a torrent, a force she couldn't deny.

'Iona,' he said, on a hard, fast note.

At long last he bent his black head and kissed her, plunging deep into her mouth with no finesse, a driving imperative that swept her into something perilously close to ecstasy. Like a conqueror, he took what he wanted in a kiss so ravishing she moaned into his mouth.

His head jerked up; he scanned her face, then gave a long jagged sigh and swivelled her around, his arms closing about her in a grip that revealed his arousal. Iona shuddered, and his grip relaxed, but she tightened the arms around his shoulders, shamelessly pressing against him and rotating her hips in slight, seductive movements.

His thick, impeded voice muttered something in Greek before he demanded, 'How the hell can I withstand such temptation?'

'Why do you want to?' she flung back at him.

He moved lightning fast, pinning her hips against his loins so she could feel their strength and the urgent hunger that possessed him. Her pulses rocketed even higher and her lashes drooped in sultry, involuntary invitation.

Luke slid his hands into her hair and tilted her head so he could stare into her eyes. Almost formally he said, 'I want two different things, and the wanting is tearing me apart. I wish to show you respect—that I value you, and am not merely using you to fulfil my own purposes. Perhaps I misjudged, but I thought making love should wait until after our wedding.'

Joy ricocheted through her, setting off small explosions of pleasure and delight. She said huskily, 'You *did* misjudge! I hope you're not one of those men who believe a bride is somehow too pure to want or enjoy sex?'

'No!' he said explosively, and laughed, his eyes glittering with appreciation. 'How is it that I never know what you're going to say next?'

'Because you don't understand women very well?'

Something hard moved in the tawny depths of his eyes, and his tone had a ring of aloofness to it. 'I have no problems with most women—it's just you who continually surprises me.' He bent a little further, so that his lips just grazed hers. Against them he said, 'I want you so very, very much. But if we make love now I will be cheating you of the wedding night you deserve...'

She shook her head. 'I won't feel cheated whatever we do,' she said shakily, adding with a hint of bite in her words, 'But if you come over all noble on me now I'm going to be seriously frustrated.'

His laughter came from deep in his throat, and he startled her by sweeping her up in his arms. 'I like it that you are so honest about your need for me,' he said, looking down into her face. His arms tightened around her as he headed towards the bedroom wing.

He carried her along the wide, shady terrace, through the scents of the night, the silvery light of the moon, into his room.

'Do you mind?' he asked, setting her down on her feet.

She looked around, remembering other nights here in this tropical ambience, all cool wood and white paint with touches of blue. 'What about Chloe?'

'I have another baby monitor in here, just in case she wakes—which she rarely does.' And then he set her down on her feet and said in a voice that came close to a growl, 'I want to ravish you, and you make the most erotic soft cries when that happens. Possibly that might wake her if we go to your room.'

Colour burned up through her skin as her blood leapt at the need that smouldered in his eyes, the dangerous note in his words. Fighting a desperate desire, she slid her hands up beneath his shirt. His skin was hot and smooth against her seeking palms, his heart thundering into her palms with a rapid, primal beat that echoed within her.

She said huskily, 'Do I?'

'Don't you remember?' he purred, and eased away so he could strip off his shirt.

It was amazing to realise what details had imprinted

themselves on her mind. Powerfully muscled, with the dusting of dark hair across his wide chest adding to his virile impact, he was all male.

Next to him she felt small and fragile, yet unafraid. 'I remember,' she whispered, and leaned up to kiss his shoulder, allowing her tongue to drift sensuously over the smooth, taut skin.

He tasted slightly salty, a flavour that was dark and delicious and entirely his own. And that simple caress made him shiver, contracted the lean muscles against her into hard, heady potency.

Excitement thrilled through Iona, voluptuous and addictive, setting her alight with a fire that had never been truly extinguished. Her breasts tightened in ardent anticipation, the nipples pressing against the fabric of her camisole, urgent and pleading.

Luke looked down. 'Yes,' he drawled wickedly, 'I can see that you do.'

He caught her close and kissed her again, mouth exploring as he tried to remove the only barrier between them.

After a few shattering seconds he tore his mouth loose and demanded, 'Is this some sort of corset? Don't tell me they're coming back into fashion?'

'No.' It was all she could think of to say; waves of shattering pleasure were tossing her higher and higher.

'Hmm, perhaps it's a pity. This is hard enough to take off and a corset would be worse, but I can imagine you in something ribboned and laced, alluring as hell and damned dangerous...'

His fingers eased the reluctant fabric upwards. 'When I saw you again in the apartment, all alabaster skin and sweet curves, I wondered why the hell I'd let you go.'

'You didn't let me go,' she managed, holding up her arms so that the garment could come over her head. 'I left.'

His hands closed for a sensuous second around her breasts before she was free of the camisole. And this time he kissed her without interruption, slowly backing her across the room until her legs met the side of the bed, and only his arms held her up. His mouth travelled the length of her throat, stopping at the intensely sensitive junction of shoulder and neck. Gently, carnally, he bit the skin there.

Adrenalin rushed through Iona, so mingled with eagerness and anticipation that she gasped and turned her head into his shoulder. Those tiny nibbling kisses gave no quarter; he had remembered the exact location of each hidden pleasure point, and set them on fire with his deliberately tormenting lips.

Astonishingly, before that too-knowing mouth had journeyed anywhere near her breasts, the preliminary signs of ecstasy sent a molten tension zinging across every nerve and cell in her body.

'What is it?' he asked against her skin, and when she shivered under an inrush of clamouring pleasure, he murmured in a voice that held both amusement and passion, 'Ah, I remember this also...' and resumed his ruthless seduction.

The ravishing tension became too much; resist as she did, she felt it ride her like a whirlwind, until the climax hit her and she collapsed, still locked in his arms.

He laughed softly and said, 'Do you know how that makes me feel?'

'Ch-cheated?' she muttered, her bones refusing to hold her upright.

'Far from it. I like…no, I *revel* in the knowledge that I can do that to you. It makes me feel ten feet tall…'

He kissed her hard then, without finesse, a fiery kiss that let her know more than any words could just how much he wanted her, then tumbled her backwards onto the bed, skilfully removing her trousers, and with them the briefs she wore beneath, so that she lay fully exposed to his heated, desirous gaze.

In a thickened voice he said, 'I suspect I am not going to be able to last long enough to give you the second round of pleasure you deserve for making me feel like that.'

'It won't matter,' she whispered, adoring him with her gaze, her lashes drooping so heavily at the stunning impact of all that untrammelled masculinity that she had to blink several times before she could lift them.

He tore off the rest of his clothes, revealing his muscled elegance, sleekly powerful, as he came down beside her. Tanned skin gleaming in the shafts of moonlight across the floor, he bent his head and kissed the peak of one flushed breast, his mouth closing over the tight, pleading nipple.

Iona's back arched off the bed, and the delicious sensations that had ebbed slightly surged back, pulsating through her as he gave his full attention to the other breast.

'You taste like honey and roses,' he said, and turned his head so that his roughened cheek swept across one over-sensitive nipple.

Iona shuddered, and he said urgently, 'I'm sorry—'

'No,' she breathed, and opened her eyes, meeting his gaze. 'It felt wonderful. Don't stop…'

'Your skin is so delicate,' he said, and kissed the track

his cheek had taken, then moved down to loop a chain of kisses around her waist.

Iona tensed, her senses tuned so exquisitely she shuddered. He took her throat, then lifted one hand, tracing from her mouth down the centre line of her body, delicately caressing the tiny hollow beneath her waist, and edging further until those knowledgeable fingers found the most sensitive part of her body.

That acute awareness gave way to a flood of heated anticipation, wine-sweet with promise; holding her breath, taut with desire, she waited.

Instead he lifted his head and said, 'You're sure?'

'So sure I might just do something drastic if you don't keep going.' Her voice was hoarse, the words coming in short gasps as her spine arched again, pushing into his hand in a silent plea.

'One of these days,' he said, wicked glints in his eyes, 'I shall find out just what you threaten me with, but for now I cannot...cannot...'

His voice died away as his fingers slid inside her. Iona stiffened at the enormous surge of molten pleasure his touch summoned, her lashes fluttering down to shut out his dark intent face.

'It's too much,' she said hoarsely.

'Look at me,' he said in a thick, goaded voice. *'Look at me.'*

His thumb brushed across her, and she arced at the bursting sweetness from the slight pressure while tiny shivers chased each other through her, each more reckless than the last.

Eyes suddenly dark, he said, 'No—not yet, Iona. Not yet. Wait for me.' And he settled his lean body over her, supporting himself on his elbows so she wasn't crushed by his weight.

Tormented by erotic craving, she felt every nerve in her body tense under a rushing overload of voluptuous sensation.

'Take me now,' Luke said on a raw, dangerous note, and thrust, making himself master of her reactions in one strong movement.

Voluptuous sensation rocketed through her, piercing her with a delight so powerful she almost fainted. Locking her arms around his powerful, sweat-slicked back, she met his fierce sexual drive as fiercely, tightening around him with demanding internal muscles.

Easily, naturally, they established a soaring rhythm, blocking out everything but the desperate, sensuous craving in each that fed off the other. Deep within Iona a divine anticipation built and built, pushing her ever closer to the mindlessness of rapture.

And then it came, a starburst of ecstasy in every cell, banishing everything but an addictive intoxication that sang through her. Luke flung back his head and she forced open her eyes, watching the starkly drawn contours of his face as he joined her in their private sensual paradise.

Slowly, slowly, she came down, his beloved weight anchoring her, safe as she hadn't been since the last time she'd been in Luke's bed, in his arms.

Without realising it she'd longed for this, and not just the torrid surrender to desire, but the comfort and security of his arms. Eighteen months ago in this bed she'd returned to the world of the senses, able to enjoy the taste of food, the scents she'd ignored, the colours and hues of life, the feel of the sea on her skin, the sounds of laughter and music and birdsong.

Now she ached to yield herself entirely to him, yet didn't dare. The sex had been mind-blowing before, but recognising her love had added an extra richness to it. She opened her eyes a slit. Luke was watching her, his mouth oddly grim, although it softened when he caught her peeping at him.

'Stop looking so guilty,' he said.

Colour burned along her cheeks. 'I've just broken the first commandment of all employees,' she replied, trying to sound bright and in control.

'Don't sleep with the boss?'

'That's the one.'

His brows lifted. 'If sleeping with the boss is forbidden, what's the commandment about marrying him?'

'I don't think that's covered in the lexicon,' she said primly, tensing as his hand drifted down to curve around one breast. Trying to ignore the little tingles of response, she went on, 'Luke, I'd better get back to my own bed. Chloe—'

'We'll hear her.' He nodded at the baby monitor. As if in answer a small snuffle emerged from it, dying into silence.

Iona said, 'I want to go back to my own room.' When he frowned she said, 'It's all been a bit too much. I need time.'

'What for?' He didn't sound angry, but he wasn't letting her go, either.

She took a deep breath. 'To regroup, I suppose,' she said honestly. 'I don't really know. Everything's happened so quickly. You overwhelm me. I'll probably get used to it, but right now I feel as though I've been dragged into a raging torrent, and although what's happened was magnificent, I need—well, to use a cliché, I need a bit of space.'

'Magnificent?' His golden eyes narrowed. 'I'm flattered.' Unembarrassed, he dropped his hand, sat up on the side of the big bed and switched on the lamp before stretching, lean muscles coiling and flexing beneath the sleek satin skin she'd marked, she noticed with another onrush of colour, with both her nails and her teeth.

He followed the direction of her shocked gaze, and drawled, 'Don't look shocked. These are honourable scars.'

She laughed and picked up a pillow, only to put it down again when the gleam in his eyes turned distinctly predatory.

Back in her room, she showered and slipped into pyjamas before checking Chloe.

She felt pleasantly exhausted, but once she'd got into her own bed she lay awake for a while, listening to the low rumble of ocean combers on the distant reef, and wished she'd stayed with Luke.

Her skin heated as she recalled his frank, sensuous appreciation of their lovemaking. He'd made her feel she was beautiful, that he found infinite pleasure in her body—but he hadn't told her he loved her.

Whereas she'd had to bite the words back several times.

So although he had been honest with her she'd not been—entirely—honest with him. And even though it hurt fiercely she had to bear the consequences of loving without having it reciprocated.

She could do it, she thought. She *could*. She'd keep her forbidden love hidden, and she'd make Chloe happy and bear his children, giving him what he wanted from her without counting the cost.

Yet as she finally slid into sleep she wondered if the price might perhaps prove too high…

That fear came back to her the next morning, when she watched Chloe on the beach, face intent and serious, while she built a magnificent sandcastle and decorated it with tiny bright shells and some long drifts of seaweed.

'Iona, who is that man?' Chloe asked, looking past her to the coconut palms behind.

Iona turned around, and one glance at the man who stood a few paces behind them told her immediately who he was. Once he too would have been as sinfully good-looking as his son, but the years had blurred his features, and he leaned heavily on a stick.

Aristo Michelakis—Luke's father.

And half an hour ago Luke had gone into the nearest town to make the final arrangements for their wedding...

Where, Iona thought as she stood up and tried to control the sick panic that kicked her in her stomach, is the bodyguard?

CHAPTER ELEVEN

IONA'S first instinct was one of sheer terror—she had to stop herself from snatching up Chloe and running. That lasted only a moment, because Luke's father was alone.

Heart still pounding in her ears, she fought for control. How had he got there?

She'd have seen him much sooner if he'd walked along the beach, and to reach them from the road meant negotiating a perimeter with a sophisticated security system.

She could worry about that later; right now she needed to speak first, so she could take control of the situation.

'Hello, Mr Michelakis,' she said smoothly. 'Luke isn't here, I'm afraid.'

Chloe left her sandcastle and came up to her, slipping her hand into Iona's, her gaze fixed on the man who had fathered her.

Iona bent down and said to her, 'Chloe, I can see Moana up by the house. Run up to her and tell her I said you need to stay with her until Luke comes back.'

Aristo Michelakis made no attempt to detain the child, not even noticing that she carefully steered well clear of him on her way up the beach. Silently Iona kept her eyes on her, until the housekeeper took Chloe's hand and drew her inside.

'You need not be so concerned,' he said abruptly. 'I have no need to steal her—I prefer to do things legally.' He waited a moment and added, 'Unlike my son. You can tell him this fake marriage isn't going to win him anything but everyone's mockery.'

To Iona's huge relief one of the bodyguards appeared in a silent rush through the wavering shadows of the palms and headed purposefully towards them.

Thank heavens the housekeeper had warned him. She said, 'I'm sorry you've come all this way to no avail. I must ask you to go now.'

'And if I do not want to go?'

Calmly, in the voice she'd use to a child having a tantrum, Iona said, 'The bodyguard will see that you do. I imagine you'd rather leave with dignity.'

He made a gesture that hinted at disdain and frustration before turning and limping away towards the palms. Iona watched him out of sight, and then drew in an uneven breath, filling starved lungs with the fresh sea air. She blinked, and set off swiftly for the house.

A kind of worried relief flooded her when she found Chloe ensconced in the kitchen, a glass of coconut milk in front of her, chattering away in what sounded like a mixture of English and French to the housekeeper.

Her face lit up when she saw Iona, but she looked past her to the doorway and asked apprehensively, 'Did the bad man go away?'

'He's not a bad man,' Iona corrected, because there was just a chance that some terrible lack in the justice system would see Chloe eventually delivered to Aristo Michelakis's custody. 'He's a grumpy man, because his leg hurts.'

Then Chloe bounced to her feet, announcing, 'Lukas is home,' and ran through the door.

After thanking Moana for caring for the child, Iona followed, catching the moment when Luke put Chloe down after her exuberant greeting.

He said to her, 'Go back to Moana now and help her make us some coffee. Iona and I want to talk to each other.' When she'd gone he transferred his gaze, hard and clear as topaz, to Iona. 'We'll go to my office.'

No tenderness in his tone, nothing but cool authority. Chilled, Iona asked sweetly, 'Is that an order?'

His brows drew together for a taut moment, then relaxed as he gave a reluctant smile. 'A request, of course.'

Iona walked into the office, trying to bolster her spirits with sturdy common sense. For heaven's sake, what had she expected—that one night of passion would turn Luke into the lover she so desperately wanted?

It wasn't going to happen. The sex was a bonus, one enjoyed by both her and Luke, but their marriage was for strictly practical reasons—and, having now met Aristo Michelakis, she fully understood why Luke had taken such a step. After that first glance he hadn't bothered to look at Chloe, much less acknowledge her.

Lukas glanced downwards. As always, Iona seemed calm and self-possessed. Except when she was in his arms. Then the wildly passionate woman was revealed, sensual and erotically charged, while she gave him everything he wanted from her—more than any other woman ever had.

'What did you think of my father?' he asked.

She said, 'I was sorry for him.'

Sorry for him? 'What do you mean by that?'

Unabashed, she shrugged, the fine cotton of her shirt

tightening around her breasts. Lukas dragged his mind away from the sudden urgent pressure in his groin and back to the matter of his father's unexpected and extremely unwelcome arrival.

'Just that,' she said, meeting his gaze without a tremor. 'He's alone, and lonely, and he hates it.'

'It is his own fault.'

She said, 'I don't suppose that ancient Greek king was particularly happy after he'd ordered his son killed and then found he was innocent.'

Surprised, Lukas let his brows shoot up, but she went on. 'When I watched your father limp away he looked old and defeated and sad.'

Lukas said abruptly, 'Ironic, isn't it? My father calls the story the doom of his house. Of course it doesn't necessarily play out the same down the years. Hippolytus's stepmother killed herself after he'd rejected her. My father's second wife only pretended to commit suicide— her overdose was carefully calculated so it would scare the hell out of everyone but not actually kill her.'

'What happened to her?'

Without attempting to hide his scorn he told her, 'She sank into deserved obscurity after he divorced her.'

Iona said, 'If your father calls the myth the doom of your house, why didn't he take in the lesson it taught?'

'Presumably for the same reason Theseus believed Phaedra, his wife—because he resented his son.' He shrugged, watching her absorb that.

'He should have been proud of you.'

Lukas said, 'He was, until about a year before he accused me. Then we quarrelled, and continued quarrelling until he had an excuse to send me away.'

'One alpha male feeling his potency diminish while

his son's increases,' she said dryly, meeting his gaze with rueful sympathy. 'You men!'

Lukas returned coolly, 'I've seen it happen with women too; a beauty who resents her daughter's growing loveliness while hers is fading.'

'Even if it is part of the human condition, that doesn't excuse your father's lack of faith.' Iona knew she wasn't getting anywhere, but she wanted to know as much about the rift as she could persuade Luke to tell her.

'Nothing would have given him greater pleasure than to see me sink into contemptible mediocrity. In fact, he banked on it,' Luke said, his tone bored. 'He was quite certain that without his backing I'd go under—and he did his best to make sure I did just that.'

'He doesn't know you very well.'

Luke showed his teeth. 'He learned. I set myself against him—and I won.' He paused. 'And by now he should understand me well enough to know that nothing and nobody will take Chloe from me if I can possibly prevent it.'

'He knows you well enough to be convinced that our marriage is a fake,' Iona said bleakly.

He smiled at her and came across the room. 'Then we'll just have to show him—and anyone else who's watching—that it's not, won't we.' It was not a question.

Iona angled her chin, met gleaming tawny eyes, and hid an odd chill in the region of her heart with a gallant smile. 'Yes,' she said quietly, and let herself be drawn into his arms.

And then all thought stopped as Luke's hard, possessive kiss submerged her in a tide of erotic promise.

Eventually, when he lifted his head and surveyed

her face with a fiercely kindling gaze, she gazed up at him.

'I'm going to enjoy being married to you very much,' he said, his voice unexpectedly raw.

She said, 'Remember how the myth ended? Theseus was reconciled to Hippolytus as he lay dying.'

Releasing her, Luke said with cold finality, 'That will not happen. And if there was ever any truth in that legend, the sentimental deathbed scene probably didn't happen either. Now, I have things to tell you.'

The civil ceremony had been organised and would take place early in the morning before the traditional wedding. 'It will be informally formal,' he said. 'This afternoon a woman will bring a selection of clothes for you to choose from.'

She blinked, but saw the point. Her wedding dress had been chosen for a romantic beach ceremony, not for one in a mayor's office.

'What on earth does one wear to an informally formal legal ceremony in the town hall?' she asked.

'I'm wearing a grey silk suit.' He gave her a swift, reassuring smile. 'Don't worry—you'll look good no matter what you wear, and the boutique owner will be able to guide you in your choice.' His tone altered. 'From the moment of signing in the mayor's office we will be legally married, but the traditional ceremony will still be held here. The gazebo will be a suitable setting, but if you want a different place tell Moana so they can decorate it.'

'I thought it was to be on the beach?'

He said curtly, 'The media have arrived. I have done what I can to make sure we are not interrupted, and have the local authorities' full co-operation, but there is a chance we could be overlooked.' He glanced at her. 'Do you want to take it?'

'No,' she exclaimed, horrified at the prospect of flashing paparazzi cameras. 'Of course not.'

He nodded. 'Is there anything you need? Any arrangements? Anything I have neglected to take into consideration?'

In spite of the passion in that kiss he had retreated into a cool aloofness that set her teeth on edge. 'I can't think of anything.'

'I would like us to feel that we can be completely honest with each other,' he said, still watching her.

How could she be honest when she was holding back the biggest truth in her life—that she loved him?

Taking a tangent, she said, 'Somehow I thought that a wedding here would be easier to organise.'

One black brow lifted. 'Marriage is too important an occasion not to be hedged about with formalities and ceremony in all societies. The wellbeing of the next generation is paramount.'

The reminder of the reason for their wedding flicked her on the raw. Foolishly, she felt like demanding, *But what about this generation?*

It was too late for second thoughts, for asking for the stars. She'd already decided that if this was all she had, it would have to be enough.

And if she didn't stop worrying the situation like a dog with a bone, she'd wreck any chance of happiness and possibly jeopardise Chloe's future.

Besides, meeting Aristo Michelakis had only reinforced Luke's decision for her; lonely and self-absorbed and spiky with bitterness, Chloe's birth father was no fit person to be guardian of any child.

'You must agree with that,' Luke said, his voice

hardening, 'or you would not have consented to marry me.'

'Of course I agree with you,' she said briskly, hoping he couldn't hear the thin, forlorn undernote to the words.

He did, but fortunately he attributed it to the wrong reason. 'Yet you still feel sorry for my father?'

'I'm afraid I do.'

He caught her hand and lifted it to his lips. 'You have a tender heart,' he said with satisfaction.

Then he said, in an entirely different voice, one so flinty and uncompromising it made her flinch, 'My father chose his own path. Possibly he regrets it now, but it is too late—he has said too many harsh things, shown too much rage, connived too long to destroy me. There will never be a reconciliation.'

When she said nothing, he finished curtly, 'It is better that way.'

'How did he get onto the beach?'

Luke frowned. 'Easily enough—he told the gate-keeper he was expected. I had given no orders that he was to be denied, and my resemblance to him meant he was given access as of right. It won't happen again.'

'Did you know he'd had you watched?'

'Of course,' he said indifferently.

Struck by another thought, Iona felt her skin crawl.

Had Aristo Michelakis learned that she and Luke had made love last night and come to see if he could frighten—or buy—her off?

Luke guessed what she was thinking. 'It's all right. I trust my staff, and he has no chance of finding out what happens here. And you needn't fear that we'll be under constant scrutiny from him. He keeps a distant eye on what I'm doing. This is the first time he's ever come onto my property or anywhere near me.'

Unconsciously she bit her lip, stopping guiltily when he said, 'Each time you do that I shall have to kiss it better.' He followed suit, pulling away far too soon, and said with a glinting smile, 'So from now on remember that whenever you chew on your lip you're asking for a kiss.'

She laughed and left it at that, but the knowledge that Aristo was having them watched was like a cold hand on her shoulder. Until it occurred to her that perhaps it was the lonely old man's way of having some connection with the son and daughter he'd abandoned.

Somewhat comforted by that, later Iona chose a sleek silk dress to wear to the mayor's office, glad that no prices were mentioned. Tahiti might be on the opposite side of the world from Paris, but the clothes she was shown were pure designer chic with a twist of tropical bravura. And had prices, no doubt, that would make her gasp.

The slim garment, pale blue and ethereal as a summer dawn, draped her body without being blatantly sexy, and high heels in the same colour meant she wouldn't look quite so short beside Luke's tall frame. The matching fascinator added a touch of frivolity and fantasy.

'You know how to pull your hair back into a chignon?' the boutique owner asked, touching her own sleekly so-phisticated hair. She gave a wide smile. 'It will show off the hat better. And your beautiful skin.'

Iona nodded, and, after practising in her bathroom with both style and fascinator, decided she agreed with the owner and would wear it like that on her wedding day.

She didn't sleep much that night. The words *wedding*

day kept echoing in her head, locking her into thoughts of a different wedding, which had been planned for New Zealand amongst family and close friends.

Gavin was now a loved memory, he and her parents no longer a source of anguish, yet she felt an aching emptiness as she lay in the luxurious room listening to the trade wind rustle through the leafy crowns of the coconut palms.

The arrival of Luke's father had upset her. She couldn't stop herself from feeling an immense sorrow for both the old man and the son he'd rejected.

Her eyes were hot and heavy, and she had a disconcerting urge to let the tears flow. Too late now, she told herself, and determinedly counted her blessings. In two days' time she'd marry the man she loved, become mother to the child she loved too. She was certain from seeing Luke with Chloe that beneath that authoritative, dominant and very Mediterranean exterior was a man who could be trusted to keep his word.

Surely that was enough? she asked herself, knowing it wasn't...

Then you're greedy, she scolded, and to escape her thoughts got up and walked across to the doors, pulling back the drapes to look out onto a tropical fantasy, softly silver-gilt and black, the full moon's rays shafting down between the palms and skimming the tiny waves as they creamed onto the milky sand.

Why hadn't Luke come to her tonight? She needed the reassurance of his passion.

From the corner of her eye she caught a movement and froze, her breath blocking her throat. Only for a second, but she didn't relax when she recognised Luke walking up from the beach, his head bent as though he was thinking deeply.

Or regretting deeply?

Iona let the drapes fall and stepped back into the darkness of her room, listening to the sound of her heart thudding unevenly against the ceaseless murmur of the waves on the reef.

The following day was so busy she and Luke barely exchanged a private word together. Early in the morning Luke drove in to pick up Angie and her children, and from then it was all noise and laughter as the two boys explored the house and beach, Chloe trotting along with them, Luke in charge.

In the afternoon more people arrived; Luke introduced her to a gorgeous Spaniard who turned out to have a name several pages long and an ancestry even longer. He was to be best man at the wedding, and although he greeted her with charming courtesy she suspected he was probably wondering how on earth someone as entirely lacking in glamour had caught Luke's eye.

A little later two couples—close friends of Luke's—flew in to celebrate the wedding with him.

People came and went; she had almost no time to talk to Luke, and in the late afternoon he left with all the guests except Angie and the children—because, of course, the bride and groom could not be allowed to see each other until they met at the wedding ceremony.

Feeling oddly abandoned, Iona showered and changed, and walked across to the bed. She'd got into it when she saw a parcel deposited on the table.

Carefully wrapped, it had her name on the outside, with *'Delivery By Hand'* written beneath in strong handwriting.

Luke? She opened the parcel with an eagerness she didn't try to restrain.

She couldn't control the shock of disappointment

when she realised it was just a magazine—one that seemed to combine gossip with interviews, and mostly featured celebrities. Titles were scattered through the pages, alongside photographs of impossibly elegant people posing gracefully in superb clothes.

'Who on earth would send me this?' she muttered, flicking through the pages. Not Luke, that was for sure; she couldn't believe he'd be interested in anything like this—

Her gaze stopped on a photograph. Luke. And a woman.

With an odd detachment Iona realised her hand was trembling. She glanced back to the cover and saw the same woman, smiling with mystery and sultry, slightly mocking invitation.

Iona dragged in a jagged breath and turned to the page. Luke's companion was utterly gorgeous, in an ethereal, fine-boned way, and she was very familiar— the newest and most beautiful Hollywood star, with a string of hit films behind her, plus rave reviews for her acting, poised on the verge of a dazzling future.

Slowly, a dark dread coalescing around her heart, Iona braced herself, turned back to the cover of the magazine and found the date. It was the latest issue.

All she wanted to do was ignore this poisoned gift from Aristo Michelakis—because of course that was who'd sent it—yet she couldn't put the magazine down. Something inside her crumpled and died as she examined the picture, noting the way Susan Mainwaring looked up at Luke, the care with which he was helping her down a step.

The caption told her they were at the opening of a new theatre in London. In what could only be called gushing prose it detailed the dress the film star was wearing, and referred readers to the next pages for an in-depth interview with her.

Summoning every bit of will she possessed, Iona forced herself to read it, and finally closed the magazine. Nausea gripped her, and a dark despair.

Not only had Susan Mainwaring made it obvious—without exactly saying so—that she expected to marry Luke, but when asked about combining a family with her glittering career she'd laughed and asserted, 'Oh, plenty of time for that in the future—if it happens. There's no room for children in my life right now, and I'm not hearing any clock ticking.'

Thereby neatly underlining that she was years younger than her nearest and greatest acting rivals.

And, from the schedule she gave, she wasn't going to have time for anything much—not even Luke—for several years yet. Certainly if she'd married Luke there would have been no place in her heart or her life for Chloe.

Although she'd been discreet, only letting a few words escape about the man in her life escape, it was clear she and Luke were lovers.

A fierce jealousy almost tore Iona apart. She had to pace around her room, her mind seething, her heart contracting into a painful lump in her chest. She could not marry Luke without knowing what promises—if any—he'd made to the film star.

Her first impulse—to call him—was dashed when she realised she didn't know how to contact him. He'd not given her a number for his cell phone. Moana had gone home for the night, and Iona didn't know the hotel phone number—wasn't even sure of the name of the place or where it was. It could be in the next bay, or halfway around the main island.

She could look it up—but would they know who she was? They might think she was a journalist. Still, she could try.

A couple of minutes later she put the telephone down. The receptionist had said politely that there was no answer from Luke's room.

She had to talk to Luke.

For a few seconds she hated his father for doing this to her; he'd gauged her well, rightly guessing she'd know she couldn't compete with Susan Mainwaring.

She said angrily, 'Horrible old man! I wish—' and stopped, because of course she didn't wish him dead.

Just out of her life—and Luke's. And Chloe's.

Driven to her feet, she unlatched the door and walked outside into the moonlight. Where was Luke when she desperately needed him?

A lovers' moon shone down, all traces of gold vanished so that the light was a pure, hard-edged white.

She stood on the edge of the terrace and shivered in spite of the warmth. Because it hurt less to think of a tragedy more than two thousand years old than to face what she'd read, she mulled over the story of doomed Hippolytus and his stepmother, Phaedra, who had wanted him and then betrayed him.

Perhaps Aristo was right when he called the story of Theseus his family's doom. Luke would do anything to safeguard Chloe, even marry a woman he didn't—perhaps could never—love.

She turned and went back inside, turning the magazine over, hopefully scanning the article to see if she could work out when the film star had been interviewed.

No clue; she didn't know anything about magazine production, but surely this interview must have occurred before Luke knew Neelie had to care for her mother?

In which case he could have been planning to marry the film star, feeling that with the constant presence of her father and Neelie an absent stepmother wouldn't harm Chloe.

She dropped the magazine as though it poisoned her.

'Think,' she said aloud, her voice fierce. '*Think*, instead of wallowing in angst.'

So how had Aristo seen the interview? Her mind worried with that question until she dismissed it. It didn't matter—someone could have told him, or he could have had a press clipping service so that anything about Luke was sent to him. What *did* matter was that this very interview could have persuaded Aristo that he had a chance of wresting Chloe away from his son. Any lawyer conducting Aristo's case would consider those airy comments on Susan Mainwaring's lack of interest in children a godsend.

Aristo Michelakis must be pretty sure Iona would be convinced. Not just convinced, but shattered enough to jilt his son.

She collapsed limply onto the side of the bed. Even to her it seemed ridiculous and irrational, but she had to know whether or not he'd made any promise to Susan Mainwaring.

And if he had...?

She set her jaw. She'd face that when she came to it. First she had to find out.

CHAPTER TWELVE

IONA finally got through to Luke late at night.

'What is it?' he demanded, his voice hard with concern. 'What is wrong?'

'I need to see you,' she told him baldly. 'It's all right—Chloe's fine.'

The pause that followed her words screwed her nerves to a point of pain, until he said in a matter-of-fact tone, 'I'll be there in ten minutes.'

Setting the phone down, she glanced across at the curtains billowing softly in the breeze and thought wildly, *He's going to think I'm mad. And this business with the magazine can only make things worse between him and his father.*

Too late now.

It didn't occur to her to pull on a dressing gown. It wasn't until Luke came noiselessly through the curtains, big and dark and dominant, that she realised she was wearing a pair of pyjamas that had seen much better days.

He said coolly, 'Is this a seduction scene, Iona?'

But his eyes had kindled and a raw note ran through the words, and she suddenly felt a little less tense. 'No,' she said raggedly, and gestured at the magazine, open on the bed. 'Read that.'

Black brows drawing together over his blade of a nose, he picked up the magazine, glanced at the cover and looked up sharply. 'Where did you get this?'

'Never mind that,' she said calmly. 'Please read it.'

Frown deepening, he scrutinised it, then dropped the magazine onto the floor. 'I suppose you want to know whether or not we were lovers.'

'Not that,' she said, muscles contracting as though she faced a blow. 'I want to know whether or not she had any right to hint at a marriage between you.'

'No.'

Just one word—so easy to say, so simple—but a word that meant more than anything else he'd ever said to her. Their eyes locked; his were dark and unsparing, and for a moment Iona wavered, and then at a purely instinctual level she understood he was telling the truth.

'That's fine, then,' she said quietly.

He stared at her. 'Is that all you need?'

'Yes.'

After a pause he said in a level voice, 'I don't know why she said that—or even if she did. Journalists have been known to get things wrong. But Susan made it obvious from the start of our affair that she wasn't looking for marriage. She certainly wanted nothing to do with Chloe while we were lovers.'

That hurt like a blow struck at her heart, but she steadied herself enough to say, 'Go on.'

He said, 'I finished our affair when I discovered my father was planning to sue for custody of Chloe. Just before we arrived in New Zealand.'

'Did you love her?' No sooner had she said the words than she longed desperately to be able to call them back. She sounded so needy. Love had no part in their bargain; she had no right to quiz him about his feelings.

He shrugged. 'No.' He paused, then said with taut irony, 'It was a very convenient affair—for us both. But Chloe comes first.'

'Of course.'

On a note of exasperation he said, 'You forget how I was brought up—to be the one to look after the family. It was always part of the deal—to behave as my father did, and his father before him.'

'Except that your father didn't,' she said in swift anger. 'He tore the family apart because he didn't believe you. He rejected you.'

Luke looked bored. 'I'm not interested in him now—or only in as much as he affects Chloe.' He glanced at the magazine and said on a steely note, 'And you.'

Iona's breath clogged into a painful lump in her chest. 'He doesn't affect me at all. No, that's not quite true—I still feel a bit sorry for him. But not sorry enough to feel you shouldn't fight him in this.'

His smile made her shiver. 'To the death. Now, why was it so important for you to hear from my lips that I had no intention of marrying Susan?'

She didn't dare confess her love for him. He waited, and when she didn't speak his brows rose. In a dry, deliberate voice he said, 'Very well. Tell me why you chose me for an affair eighteen months ago.'

A cautious glimmer of hope smouldered into life. She took a jagged breath, then with a rashness that startled her, risked everything. 'You're so alive, so much in control of your life, and so strong. That's what drew me to you at first. And when you made it obvious that for you it would only be a holiday affair—nothing serious, just fun and pleasure and brilliant sex—I thought it was perfect. But I only wanted to be healed, not to fall in love.'

Still he didn't turn. It was like talking to a statue. Heart in her mouth, she heard him speak.

'I was a fool.'

She could gain nothing from his tone—cool, flat, without expression. She said, 'No, I was the fool. When you suggested we keep up the affair, that I live with you, I was afraid of being hurt all over again.'

At last he turned, his face set and frowning like one of the old gods of his country. 'Why, for heaven's sake?'

'I refused to admit it, but I was falling in love all over again, and this time it wasn't the sweet boy-girl thing I'd had with Gavin. It was powerful and frightening and heart-wrenching. And I knew...'

Her voice trailed away into a silence that held her still.

'You knew what?' he rasped.

Inwardly quivering, she forced the words out. 'That last night, after you'd asked me to live with you, I dreamed that I was married to Gavin, and you arrived and said, "Come," and I left him, running towards you with such joy, such happiness.'

'You left me because of a *dream*?' he demanded incredulously.

'No, not that, but because it showed me something I hadn't faced until then.'

'And that was?' When she didn't answer immediately he commanded ruthlessly, 'Tell me, Iona.'

She was horrified to find she was wringing her hands. Hastily putting them behind her, she whispered, 'Oh, it sounds so *stupid*. I left you because I was a coward.'

Luke came towards her, stopping a mere pace away.

She didn't dare lift her eyes further than the small pulse of a muscle in his jaw.

In a deep, quiet voice he said, 'Like me, you had learned in a hard school that love can be followed by disaster. Why did you believe me when I told you I had not slept with my father's wife?'

Iona stared at him. 'I...I told you before. I can't give you an exact reason beyond sheer gut instinct,' she said unevenly. 'I just *know* you wouldn't do that.'

'You must also know that I have had several lovers—none of whom I've married—and been credited with many more. Such a man could be one who takes women lightly, uses them, then discards them. Why didn't you believe that of me?'

'Because it isn't in you to behave like that,' she said instantly.

'I forced you into looking after Chloe, bulldozed you into this marriage.' His gaze raked her face, intent, compelling. 'What makes you think I would not force my father's wife into my bed?'

'You never call her your stepmother.'

'She was an insult to the word *mother*. Why do you not believe the lies she told? Because I can make you weep with ecstasy in bed? Because I am far richer than my father?'

'No,' she told him quietly. 'Because I've seen you with Chloe. And...' She stumbled, searching for words.

'Tell me, Iona.'

'I just *know*,' she repeated in confusion, because she couldn't give him the reason he seemed to want.

'Just as you knew that with me you'd find life and rapture again?'

'Yes.' And then, more bravely, 'Yes. I'm sorry I can't be more explicit than that. You wear your honour, your integrity, your strength like a banner.' Still he said nothing, and she finished in a tired voice. 'Which sounds stupid, I know—'

'It sounds magnificent,' he interrupted swiftly, and smiled, and she realised with a soaring heart that he believed her.

Oh, they hadn't solved everything—he hadn't even mentioned the word she longed to hear—but perhaps, in time, he would learn to love her...

Thoughtfully he said, 'The ancient Greeks had the right idea when they ascribed love to Eros, a wayward child who shot arrows into people's hearts for the sheer mischief of it. I think there is a little more logic to it than that, but I have to admit I fell in love with you when I first saw you walking along the beach out there, your long hair blowing in the trade wind. You looked like a Botticelli angel come down to earth—a wistful angel who wanted nothing more than oblivion.'

Speechless, hardly able to believe her ears, she lifted her gaze, saw a warmth in his tawny eyes that held something of passion, but even more of love.

'I'd like you to say that again,' she whispered.

He laughed deep in his throat. 'Only if you reciprocate. I am too Greek to take any pleasure in vowing love if you don't feel the same way.'

'Oh, Luke,' she said on a broken sigh, 'you must know I do.'

'Do what?'

His voice was amused, but the dark heat in his eyes had flared into fire and she said fiercely, 'Do *love* you, you idiot. Of *course* I love you—I think it must have happened that first day too, when you ordered me off your beach and then made me sit down and drink something before driving me back to my hotel. You've been part of me ever since.'

'Which is why you fled from me as soon as I asked you to stay with me?' he said austerely, and as she opened her mouth he held up his hand. 'No, I understand. I *do* understand. To love someone and then lose him is a tragedy, and your parents' deaths so soon afterwards…' He made a quick gesture. 'My own mother's death was tragedy enough for me.' He paused, then said sombrely, 'And for my father.'

After a quick glance at his watch, he looked at her, his expression stripped of everything except naked longing. 'A declaration of love should be sealed with a kiss—but I don't dare touch you, let alone kiss you.'

For the first time Iona let herself believe that what he felt for her was all that she'd ever wanted—no, she thought with breaking joy, *more* than she'd ever wanted. He couldn't look at her with such intensity, such open hunger and tenderness, and not mean it.

'Why?' she asked.

'It is too close to midnight for what I want to do— ravish you for hours—and Angie is convinced we're wooing the very worst of bad luck if we set eyes on each other before our wedding tomorrow.'

Iona choked back a laugh. 'I'm prepared to risk it if you are.'

He took a half-step towards her, then stopped. 'I can wait,' he said heroically. 'The first time after we have declared our love should not be hurried. Tomorrow will be our wedding night and we can make love all night long—if I can stand it.'

Frustration drummed through her in a driving crescendo. 'I love you,' she said.

He stiffened, and for a moment she thought he was

coming towards her. However, he stepped back and said roughly, 'I am only too human where you are concerned! I'll go now. But tomorrow—this time tomorrow…'

Although he left the sentence unfinished, his smile and the swift golden glitter in his eyes sent a shiver of sheer delight and need through her.

'Luke…'

Luke slid a questing hand from her hip to the soft curve of her breast. 'What is it, my dear one?'

'Earlier today, just as we were all getting ready for the garden wedding, Chloe asked if she could call me Mama.'

The slow sensuous movement of his hand stilled. 'And you said…?'

'I said she could.'

He lifted her chin and kissed her, long and tender and passionate, then tucked her head into his shoulder.

'I hadn't realised she felt the need for a mother.' He kissed her and said, 'You have given her something Neelie was never quite able to be for her.'

'I've been thinking about Neelie,' she said. 'She might not be openly motherly, but I'm sure she learned to love Chloe.'

'Of course.' He sounded slightly surprised.

'Do you think she'd like to be a grandmother?' When he said nothing she went on, 'Chloe has no grandmothers. And I'm sure she'd like to see Neelie whenever we're in the UK, just as Neelie must want to keep in touch with her.'

He said quietly, 'You fill my heart with your sweetness. Yes, of course we must make sure Neelie is part of our family.' He paused, then went on, 'And now I have something to tell you. Two things, in fact. This morning—before the official ceremony—my father came to see me.'

She stiffened in his arms, then tilted her head back so she could see his face against the pillow, dark and saturnine. She could read nothing from his expression. 'Why?' she breathed.

'To tell me he'd sent a letter to his lawyers instructing them he no longer planned to sue for custody of Chloe.'

Dumbfounded, she stared at him.

He watched her with a lurking smile, then said, 'I think this is the first time I've ever seen you without a word to say.'

'Why—what...? What made him change his mind?'

'He had never seen her before. She looks like my mother. And he loved my mother deeply; he was desolated when she died.'

He stretched, but when she moved to give him room he pulled her back into his arms, leaning his head on top of hers as her body curved against the hard contours of his. 'I like the way your hair falls in a curtain across me,' he murmured lazily. 'Such warm, living silk. As he had sent the magazine to you, it did occur to me his unexpected surrender was made so that I could pull out of the wedding if I wanted to—which would prove I was only marrying to safeguard Chloe.'

She asked hesitantly, 'Do you think that is the reason?'

'Strangely enough, no. Apparently you—although you do *not* look like my mother—also reminded him of her.'

Stunned, she demanded, 'How?'

'My mother was forthright, loving, and not afraid

to speak her mind.' He finished a little roughly, 'He said that she would have liked you. And he's right—she would have.'

Iona curved her hand around his jaw, relishing the soft abrasion, the warmth that beat from his skin. 'I feel as though some heavy weight has been lifted off my shoulders. Is this the end, do you think?'

'Perhaps the beginning of the end,' he said.

She twisted up onto her elbow and looked down at him, her gaze caressing the beloved contours of his face. 'How do you feel about that?'

His shoulders moved in the nearest approach to a shrug he could manage in bed. 'I didn't start it,' he said evenly. 'I never attacked him; I merely blocked his moves to bring me down. If at any time he'd come to me and told me he was ready to make an end to it, I'd have welcomed it.'

'And now?'

Luke thought for a moment, then said slowly, 'It will take time, but I hope we can build on the ruins of our old relationship. I think he has realised that he is the only one being hurt by his refusal to accept me.'

She nodded. 'You said you had something else to tell me?'

He frowned, then gave a sardonic smile. 'I was jealous of Iakobos.'

'*What?*'

He laughed wryly. 'Yes. You and he seemed to like each other, and I was so jealous I sent him away.'

'You had no reason,' she protested, still dazed at such a confession.

'I know,' he admitted cheerfully. 'And it will not affect his career. I did not believe myself to be a jealous man, but I realised that I have it in me. It was a shock—a salutary one.'

His arm tightened and effortlessly he brought her down to lie on his chest. Iona shivered as his body stirred, hardened beneath her. In a thickened voice he said, 'I will not make your life miserable with jealousy, and I will always protect you and cherish you and tell you the truth. And always, dear heart, *always* I will love you—with all that I am, everything I have.'

Her tears fell onto his chest, and he said in a shaken voice, 'What have I said to make you cry?'

'I'm crying because I'm so happy.' She wiped the tears away and bent to kiss him. 'I will always love you, and tell you the truth too—even when you don't want me to,' she added.

He laughed. 'I know that,' he said with satisfaction and kissed her again, and once more she felt the sweet hunger, the passionate love she was at last free to express.

She lifted her head and kissed him again, lips lingering on a swell of muscle, the sound of his increasing heartbeat music in her ears.

'Mmm, you taste good,' she whispered against his skin.

'So do you.'

Luke would always fire out orders, organise lives, rule his empire with formidable authority, but she had known from the moment she'd seen him that he was so much more than a dominant male. She and Chloe and any children they might have would be safe in his love.

As his hand traced the curve of her breasts, the narrow indentation of her waist, the flare of her hips, she sighed and whispered, 'You'll have to teach me how to say *I love you* in Greek.'

'Later,' he said, laughter catching in his throat. 'Much, much later...'

And then, locked together in passion that had been transformed so stealthily into love, they found the heaven that would always be theirs in each other's arms.

Coming Next Month

from **Harlequin Presents®**. Available October 26, 2010.

Coming Next Month

from **Harlequin Presents® EXTRA.** Available November 9, 2010.

LARGER-PRINT BOOKS!

HARLEQUIN *Presents*~

PASSION GUARANTEED SEDUCTION

GET 2 FREE LARGER-PRINT NOVELS PLUS 2 FREE GIFTS!

YES! Please send me 2 FREE LARGER-PRINT Harlequin Presents® novels and my 2 FREE gifts (gifts are worth about $10). After receiving them, if I don't wish to receive any more books, I can return the shipping statement marked "cancel." If I don't cancel, I will receive 6 brand-new novels every month and be billed just $4.55 per book in the U.S. or $5.24 per book in Canada. That's a saving of at least 13% off the cover price! It's quite a bargain! Shipping and handling is just 50¢ per book.* I understand that accepting the 2 free books and gifts places me under no obligation to buy anything. I can always return a shipment and cancel at any time. Even if I never buy another book, the two free books and gifts are mine to keep forever.

176/376 HDN E5NG

Name	(PLEASE PRINT)	
Address		Apt. #
City	State/Prov.	Zip/Postal Code

Signature (if under 18, a parent or guardian must sign)

Mail to the **Harlequin Reader Service**:
IN U.S.A.: P.O. Box 1867, Buffalo, NY 14240-1867
IN CANADA: P.O. Box 609, Fort Erie, Ontario L2A 5X3

Not valid for current subscribers to Harlequin Presents Larger-Print books.

**Are you a subscriber to Harlequin Presents books
and want to receive the larger-print edition?
Call 1-800-873-8635 today!**

* Terms and prices subject to change without notice. Prices do not include applicable taxes. Sales tax applicable in N.Y. Canadian residents will be charged applicable provincial taxes and GST. Offer not valid in Quebec. This offer is limited to one order per household. All orders subject to approval. Credit or debit balances in a customer's account(s) may be offset by any other outstanding balance owed by or to the customer. Please allow 4 to 6 weeks for delivery. Offer available while quantities last.

HPLP10R

HARLEQUIN®

A Romance

FOR EVERY MOOD™

Spotlight on

Inspirational

Wholesome romances
that touch the heart and soul.

See the next page
to enjoy a sneak peek from
the Love Inspired® Suspense
inspirational series.

"It's okay. I'm here to help." The voice was as deep as the darkness, but Jenna Dougherty didn't believe the lie. She could do nothing but lie still as hands slid down her arms, felt the rope around her wrists.

"I'm going to use a knife to cut you free, Jenna. Hold still."

The cold blade of a knife pressed close to her head before her gag fell away.

"I—" she started, but her mouth was dry, and she could do nothing but suck in air.

"Shhh. Whatever needs to be said can be said when we're out of here." Nick spoke quietly, his hand gentle on her cheek. There and gone as he sliced through the ropes on her wrists and ankles.

He pulled her upright. "Come on. We may be on borrowed time."

"I can't leave my friend," Jenna rasped out.

"There's no one here. Just us."

"She has to be here." Jenna took a step away.

"There's no one here. Let's go before that changes."

"It's dark. Maybe if we find a light…"

"What did you say?"

"We need to turn on the light. I can't leave until I know that—"

"What can you see, Jenna?"

"Nothing."

"No shadows? No light?"

"No."

"It's broad daylight. There's light spilling in from the window I climbed in through. You can't see it?"

She went cold at his words.

"I can't see anything."

"You've got a nasty bruise on your forehead. Maybe that has something to do with it." His fingers traced the tender flesh on her forehead.

"It doesn't matter *how* it happened. I'm blind!"

Can Nick help Jenna find her friend or will chasing this trail have Jenna running blindly again into danger?

Find out in RUNNING BLIND, available in November 2010 only from Love Inspired Suspense.